AIDEN

SAN FRANCISCO SHOCKWAVES
BOOK 2

SAMANTHA LIND

SAMANTHALIND.COM

Aiden
San Francisco Shockwaves Book 2
Copyright 2022 Samantha Lind
All rights reserved
Print ISBN: 978-1-956970-09-8

Cover Design by Jersey Girl Design
Cover image by Wander Aguiar
Cover Model Camden
Editing by *Amy Briggs ~ Briggs Consulting LLC*
Proofreading by *Proof Before You Publish*

❀ Created with Vellum

CONTENTS

CHAPTER 1
TORI

I sit on my best friend Avery's couch. We just got back from her new boyfriend, Ryker's, hockey game. The first one I've ever been to in my life. It was incredibly intense. The effortless way the guys are on their skates is impressive; add in the way they throw their bodies around, pushing one another into the glass, makes my own body ache.

"Hey, Ryker wants to know if we want to meet up with the guys at a bar?" Avery asks as she enters the apartment after taking her dog, Max, out for a walk.

"Sure, it sounds like fun," I tell her as Max jumps on the couch next to me and tries to lick my face. "No, Max," I correct and push him away. I rub the top of his head, and he calms down, accepting the love I'm willing to give him. "When do we need to leave?" I ask.

"Now, they're all headed there already."

"Let me just use the bathroom, and I'm good to go," I tell her as I try and hide a yawn behind my hand.

"If you're tired, we can stay here," Avery offers.

"I'm good; it will help me with the jet lag. I'm trying hard to get back on my normal schedule. I have to go back to work in a few days and need to be ready to get into the groove again," I remind her.

"Okay, if you need to leave at any time, just let me know, and we can go. I'm going to check in with Ellie, and I'll be ready to go," she says.

"How about I just drive? I can leave when I'm ready and go straight home. You can ride back with Ryker, right?"

"Of course; sounds like the perfect plan." She claps her hands together excitedly as she heads out the door.

I stay put while she goes next door to Ryker's condo, checking in on his teenage daughter, Ellie. Ellie is the main reason Ryker and Avery have become so close the last few weeks. She's a pretty cool kid, not one of those bratty or bitchy teenagers. I enjoyed hanging out with her tonight, plus, it was cool to have someone so knowledgeable about the game explaining what was happening down on the ice to us.

"So, are you looking to hook up with a hockey player tonight?" Avery asks once we're in my car and on our way to the bar.

"No, but I look forward to meeting them." I smirk. "If they look half as good as Ryker did in his suit, I'm sure we're in for a whole lot of suit porn tonight."

"Suits are required to and from the games; not sure if they can ditch them yet, but we'll find out soon enough." She smirks from the passenger seat as we speed down the interstate.

We walk into the bar, and it isn't packed, but also

not empty, by any means. We spot Ryker across the bar, sitting at a table with a few others around with Reserved signs on them. We walk over unnoticed until we reach the table, and Avery speaks up, "Hey," she says, getting his attention.

"Hey, yourself," he replies and gets up to come around the table. He pulls Avery into his arms. "How was the drive?" he asks.

"Fine, not that bad since it's a Sunday night," she says.

"Good," he says when a commotion near the front entrance grabs our attention. "And we've been spotted," he adds.

"Did you think you'd be able to fly under the radar?" she asks, laughter filling her voice.

"I was riding the wave as long as it lasted, but knew as soon as more guys arrived, my luck would dwindle."

"I'm sure you'll be just fine," she assures him. He whispers something into her ear, and she replies, only for him to reply back and a blush to fill her cheeks. I can only imagine what dirty things he just said to make her blush red, but I love it for my best friend.

"Ryker," a deep voice bellows as a sexy as sin man approaches. The timbre of his voice has my thighs clenching together, wondering what he'd sound like in bed talking dirty to me.

"Aiden," Ryker replies, matching his enthusiasm. They pull one another into a man hug, before releasing and stepping back from one another. "Let me introduce you," Ryker states. "This is Avery," he says as he tugs her just a little closer to his side, I'm sure in a *she's mine* gesture all of the guys recognize. "And this is her best friend, Victoria."

"You can call me Tori," I speak up quickly. I don't really like going by my full name but allow it for a few people.

"Nice to meet you," Aiden replies, and takes my hand. He brings my hand up to his lips and kisses my knuckles. My knees just about buckle from underneath me as his lips connect with my skin. They are the softest lips I've encountered on a man, and now I can't get the idea out of my head of what they'd feel like elsewhere on my body.

"Likewise," I finally get out, remembering my manners. "Are you a hockey player, as well?" I stupidly ask.

"Yeah, I play on the same line as Ryker," he says, like I should know what he means.

"Oh, cool," I once again stupidly answer. "Today's game was my first one ever, so I'm still lost as to what was going on."

"Did you enjoy it?" Ryker asks.

"I did. Ellie was incredibly helpful, trying to explain all the calls and what was happening."

"She's a pretty smart one," Ryker states.

"I'm sure I could answer any of your burning questions about the game," Aiden says. Is that a smolder I see in his gaze? He's stayed close since our introduction. His body wash or aftershave has quite the boldness to it. I'd love nothing more than to bury my face in his chest and take in a deep breath. It's intoxicating and I could quickly get drunk on his smell alone.

Avery moves to take a seat, so I follow suit. Aiden sits down next to me, and the contact our legs make sends chills down my spine.

"Cold?" he whispers in my ear.

I can't help the small smile from forming as I turn my head his way. "No, just got a single chill when I sat down."

His smirk tells me he doesn't believe it was just a chill, but there's no reason to tell him more, at this point. I'm sure he's a playboy. He's got a confidence about him demonstrating, one, he knows he's good-looking; two, he knows he's got the fame card in his pocket; and three, he could probably take any woman in this bar home tonight if he asked.

"Let's do shots!" one of the other guys calls out as the server arrives with a tray filled with them. Both Avery and I decline one but watch as most of the guys take them and sling them back.

"You okay?" I ask Aiden as he hits his chest with a closed fist after swallowing down the liquid.

"Yeah, just burns a little," he says. "I'll be all right."

"Sorry for the wait; here's the menu you asked for," the server says as he hands one over to Ryker. He puts in an order for some food. "I'll get everything put in right away. Can I get anyone else something?" he asks.

"I'll take a Coke," Avery tells him.

"Same for me, please," I add.

"Perfect, I'll be right back," he says before retreating from our group.

We get caught up talking with the group of guys, along with a few of their wives and girlfriends. I'm a little shocked at how nice and welcoming they all are, since I'm definitely the outsider in this group.

I find myself scooting over with Aiden as we get pulled into conversations further down the row of tables. Before I know it, I'm no longer near Avery, but at this point, it would be weird to get up and go over to where she's at; plus, I'm having a great time, so I stay put.

"Hey, Ryker and I are going to take off. Are you good?" Avery asks after she approaches the table.

"I'm good; I'll probably head out, myself, in just a few minutes," I tell her.

"Okay, call me tomorrow?" she asks. Her eyes flick between me and Aiden, and I can tell she's wondering what's going on with how close we're sitting with one another. His arm has been firmly planted behind me for a while now, his thumb tracing circles on my shoulder every once in a while.

"Of course. I've got an appointment in the morning, but I could bring lunch over?" I suggest.

"Sounds like a date," she says, and leans down for a quick hug. "Be careful; love you, Tori," she whispers in my ear.

"Love you, too. Don't pull a muscle getting freaky with your man," I retort, but don't miss her smirk.

"Are you having a good time tonight?" Aiden asks once Avery is gone.

"I am; I wasn't sure what to expect, but it's been

fun," I tell him as I yawn again, not doing a good job of hiding it.

"Tired?" he asks.

"Yeah, I'm still adjusting back to Pacific time. I was gone for six weeks in Africa on a humanitarian trip. I just got home a few days ago."

"Wow, what did your trip consist of?" he asks, and I can tell he's actually interested in my answer and not just asking to ask.

"Since we aren't medical providers, we were there to distribute supplies we brought. Everything from bottled water, first aid supplies, clothing, and some building materials. Other organizations will take medical providers over to treat people, but that wasn't our mission."

"Very cool. I take it you had a good time?" he asks.

"I did, it was so eye opening, just how good we have it here. The poverty levels we saw were heartbreaking. I wanted to help everyone, even if it wasn't a possibility."

"I can only imagine."

"It was hard the first week or so, but after that, you almost become desensitized to the conditions you're seeing constantly. Don't get me wrong, I still wanted to help every single person, especially all the kids, but we just didn't have the resources to do so. We allocated so much of our supplies for each day, and once they were gone they were gone."

"I can see how it would be hard; do you plan to go back?" he asks.

"Maybe in a few years. My boss is a big supporter of

the organization, and they send groups of people a few times a year, so it would be easy to sign up for another one. Anyone at the company who goes is still paid their normal salary without being required to use vacation to go, so it isn't an issue getting the time off. "

"Sounds like you have an amazing boss," he says.

"Yeah, I'm pretty lucky," I tell him.

"What do you do?" he asks.

"I'm the VP of marketing for a record label."

"Damn, so you work with musicians and their bands then, promoting tours and such?"

"I do, along with the marketing strategies for releasing singles or full albums. I have a four-person team who's also very hands-on."

"Sounds cool. Do you work in one genre specifically or all of them?"

"As the VP, I work with all of them, at this point. When I first started with the record label, I was assigned to one team and moved up the ranks over time. I was promoted to VP earlier this year, so I'm still getting used to being everyone's boss."

"Who's the best client you've worked with? Is it okay for me to ask?"

"Yeah." I chuckle. "Just don't ask for any dirt on anyone. While I have lots, I'm not one to spill the tea on our clients. Most are like family to me, and I just couldn't throw them under the bus. But back to your question. My absolute favorite client I work with is Reese Blackwood. Now that I think of it, you might know her husband; he plays hockey in Indianapolis."

"Austin," Aiden says, as I think about the "it"

couple in the league.

"Yes, he's so sweet and her biggest cheerleader. I love getting to spend time with them."

"Ryker has mentioned them a few times since he got to know them when he played there last season. I only know him from when I've played against him while we've both been in the league."

"I didn't realize he knew them," I tell him honestly. "I only met Ryker earlier today, before the game. I go away for six weeks and return to my best friend falling head over heels for some hockey-playing hunk."

"Head over heels, huh?" he asks, bumping into me with his shoulder.

"Oh yeah, she's a goner for him, but seeing how he looks at her, I think he's just as smitten with her as she is with him."

"I'd have to agree. He's been a pretty chipper guy, lately. I can only attribute his attitude to Avery. What about you? Are you seeing anyone?" he asks.

"Nope, been single for a while now. What about you?" I ask.

"Single, but not opposed to settling down with the right woman," he tells me.

"And what makes a woman the 'right' one?" I ask using air quotations.

"Someone who becomes my best friend. The one person I want to call first with the good and bad news, or have her call me first with her good or bad news. The one person I'd be willing to move heaven and earth for to make their life easier. Someone who wants to see me succeed and reach my own life goals and share in the excitement. Someone who can withstand the attention I sometimes get due to my job and social engagement's that are required."

"Wow, a little deeper than I was expecting," I admit.

"What were you expecting?" he asks.

"I guess I was thinking it was more going to be all about looks and how freaky she is in bed," I tell him, not backing down from the eye contact we've made.

"Don't get me wrong, a strong sexual connection is important, but it isn't the only important aspect of a relationship. Kinks can be explored in time; you don't have to jump right to whips and chains on the first date." He smirks. "Unless you're trying to give me some hints." He practically eye fucks me as the sentence falls from his lips.

"No," I stammer. He's gotten me all messed up, thinking about him naked and in bed. I can't get the idea out of my head of him controlling the encounter, my body coming to life as the thoughts flash through my mind. My clit throbs, yet I can't seem to find any relief, no matter how I shift my legs in search of just a thread of it.

"You okay there?" Aiden asks, his gravelly voice back.

"Yeah, I'm fine. But I should probably go. I need to get to bed," I tell him as I jump up from the table.

"Are you sure you're okay?" he asks as he grabs my arm, just above my elbow, as he stands behind me.

"I'm sure, just need to get home," I try and assure him. I don't mention it's to pull out my trusty vibrator to take care of things. Things he's inspired.

"Okay. I'd love to see you again, can we exchange numbers and maybe go out sometime soon?" he asks. I think about his offer, but don't know what I want with this sexy man standing in front of me. I know his type. It's all about the chase. They are players. They know the game. Can I put my heart on the line like that?

"I don't know, Aiden. I'm sure you're a great guy, but I'm not looking to date a player," I tell him. "I've got a lot on my plate with this promotion, and I can't get distracted right now."

"Let me set something straight; I might play a sport for a living, but I'm not a player off the ice." He stands to his full height, a sternness to his voice that makes me think I've offended him with my brush off."

"I'm sorry, I didn't mean to offend you. Can we just be friends, for now?" I ask, offering a small olive branch.

"I'd like that," he says. "As long as friends can text each other and hang out sometimes."

"Friends can definitely text, call, or hang out," I agree. I pull out my cell, opening my contacts and typing in his first name. "What is your last name? I realized Ryker only introduced us by our first names earlier."

"Fox," he tells me, and I type it in.

"Is it why some of the guys were calling you Foxy?" I ask, my nose scrunched a little.

"Yeah." He chuckles. "Hockey players are notorious for their nicknames. With a last name like Fox, I've been called Foxy for as long as I can remember."

"What's Ryker's?" I ask, curious about this tradition.

"Most guys call him Cap since he's our captain."

"Makes sense," I tell him as I hand over my phone for him to type in his number. He clicks a few times, then pulls out his own phone, where I see a text message waiting on the screen. When he hands my phone back, I noticed he's texted himself so he has my number already.

"And your last name?" he asks as he sets up my contact information.

"Ferguson," I tell him before spelling it out, because many people get it wrong.

"Tori Ferguson. I like the way it rolls off the tongue," he says, and my mind flicks right to the thought of him saying my name as he comes.

"If you don't quit giving me those fuck me eyes, I'm not going to be able to say goodbye to you at your car door tonight," he says as he leans in. "You don't hide your desire for me very well, Ms. Ferguson."

"Goodnight, Aiden," I tell him as I push away from him. I'm so embarrassed he's called me out like this, but I also can't stop my body's reaction to him. He's that intoxicating, and this pull I feel between the two of us is strong. I'll have to keep it in mind before I agree to another in-person meet up with him.

CHAPTER 2
AIDEN

I KICK THE COVERS OFF, STRETCHING MY SORE AND TIRED body. I need to get in a yoga session to help with the tightness I'm feeling. The start of the season is always a shock to the system. Not that I don't keep in shape year round, but there's just something different about how playing day in and day out can take its toll on the body.

My cell rings on the nightstand, so I reach over and grab it. Amy's smiling face fills the screen, so I quickly swipe to answer her call.

"Hey," I greet, my voice still filled with sleep.

"Good morning, sunshine," my sister sing-songs.

"You're chipper this morning," I point out.

"Of course I am. I'm going to the spa in an hour, thanks to your credit card. Then, getting all glammed up after."

"I think the part you like the most is the fact my credit card is paying for everything today," I muse.

"I'll never turn down a spa day at your expense.

Trust me, no woman would, so remember that whenever you finally find someone to settle down with."

"You're expensive enough, I don't know if I could handle two women in my life," I joke with my sister.

"Please," she says, and I can just see her eyeroll. "You could afford to send me to the spa every day and it wouldn't make much of a dent in your yearly contract."

"Possibly." I stand up and stretch again before heading out into the kitchen to turn the coffee pot on. "What time will you be ready for me to pick you up?"

"I should be ready by about four."

"And I'm picking you up at the spa, or back at your place?" I ask.

"The spa. I'm doing everything there, including getting dressed."

"Okay, see you then. Don't spend too much of my money," I tease her.

"Challenge accepted, big brother." She laughs before we hang up.

I agreed to a charity appearance and know Amy loves going to those types of events with me as my plus one. Until I have someone in my life I can take as my actual date, Amy it is. The thought of Tori all dressed up and on my arm flashes in my mind. The sparks I felt between the two of us the other night weren't one sided, by any means, but I also didn't miss the fact she was actively trying to put up a wall between the two of us. I just don't know why.

"AIDEN, OVER HERE," SOMEONE CALLS OUT AS AMY AND I stand along the red carpet. Camera flashes go off from everywhere. We slowly make our way down, stopping every few feet to pose for everyone, hoping we're turning in the right directions. We finally make it to the end of the carpet where a few reporters are stationed. "Aiden, can we get an interview?" one of the reporters asks.

Amy and I step aside so we're no longer blocking the main walkway for other attendees. "Sure, where would you like me?" I ask, knowing they'll want me in front of the camera.

"Stand on the X on the ground and you'll be perfect," the camera guy tells me.

I do as asked before looking at the reporter.

"Thanks for agreeing to the interview, I'm Melissa," the reporter introduces herself.

"Nice to meet you," I reply, flashing her my trademark smile I know drives most women crazy.

I don't miss the blush filling her cheeks, but she does a good job of not letting it affect her professionalism. "We've got a treat for you tonight. One of the stars of our newest professional sports team, the Shockwaves, Aiden Fox, is here with us. Mr. Fox, thank you for joining us," Melissa says as she turns her attention from the camera to me.

"Thanks for having me. You can call me Aiden." I wink at her, hoping it helps make this more comfortable. I hate stuffy and uncomfortable interviews and can usually tell when a reporter is nervous.

"Aiden." She says my name and pauses for a second

before continuing with her question. "What made you come out tonight to support the Big Brothers Big Sisters charity?"

"I've always tried to give back to my community, and kids are the heart of most communities. Making sure at-risk youth have what they need to excel in life is important, and I'm happy to support the causes."

"That's great to know you like to be involved in your community. Have you adjusted well to San Francisco?"

"I'd like to think I have. I haven't been here for long, but I've explored a little in some of my downtime. During the season, I tend to get hyper-focused on the game, so my downtime is limited. It might be next summer before I can really get out and explore."

"What's your outlook on the season?" she asks.

"One game at a time. It's obviously our goal to win as many games as possible, but as the newest team to the league, we've got a lot to overcome to be successful. Thankfully, we have great leadership who will guide us in the right direction."

"Wonderful, great to hear. Thank you for your time tonight, I hope you enjoy the event," Melissa says as she ends the interview.

"Of course, thank you," I tell her before the light above the camera shuts off, signaling it isn't recording anymore.

I step out of the interview spot. "Thank you again," Melissa says to me.

"Anytime," I tell her before I walk away with Amy on my arm.

We make our way inside, where the ballroom is decorated to the nines. They've gone all out on tonight's event, which doesn't surprise me as this is one of their largest fundraisers each year, from what I was told when invited.

Amy and I snake our way through the tables until we find ours. There are already a few people sitting at it, not many I recognize, so after introductions are made, we head for the bar to grab a drink.

The evening is fun. The program they planned did what they intended and had everyone pulling out their checkbooks to donate money. Add in the large room they had set up with silent auction items, and they'll be rolling in the cash to support their cause this year.

"Did you have fun?" Amy asks once we're back in my car and headed out of the venue.

"I did, how about you?" I ask her as I navigate the downtown traffic.

"So much fun, but you know I enjoy going to events like this one with you."

"Are you coming to my game tomorrow?" I ask.

"That is my plan, but I probably won't hang out afterward. My flight back home is early the following morning, so I want to go back to the hotel and get to bed so I have at least a few hours of sleep before my early wake up call."

"Do you need a ride to the airport?" I ask. Amy decided she wanted to stay at a hotel rather than my condo so she was closer to the touristy area and could go out and explore when I was busy during her few-day trip out to see me and attend the event with me tonight.

"I'm good. The hotel has a free shuttle and I'm already signed up to take it over. Plus, it would be way out of your way to come all the way over here to take me so early in the morning. You need your beauty sleep." She smirks at me.

"I'd forgo sleep to pick you up," I contest.

"I don't want to be blamed because you're dragging ass on the ice."

"I wouldn't drag ass, but if you want to take the shuttle, I won't stop you. Just make sure you come say goodbye before you leave the arena."

"That I can do," she confirms as I pull into the hotel's parking lot.

I park and kill the engine. I get out of my car, meeting my sister in front of it before escorting her inside. "Do you want to stop at the bar before heading up to your room?" I offer as we walk through the door being held open by an employee.

"If you want to," she says, looking at me over her shoulder.

"Let's stop for a quick drink," I tell her, and lead her to the bar. We enter and see an open table for two, so head to it.

"Evening, what can I get for the two of you tonight?" a cocktail waitress asks as she approaches the table.

"A glass of your house white," my sister says.

"Perfect, and for you, Sir?" she asks me.

"I'll just take a glass of the blonde you have on tap."

"Sixteen ounce or twenty-four?" she asks.

"Sixteen will be fine," I answer.

"Did you want anything to eat tonight?" she asks.

"I'm good, you?" I ask Amy.

"Do you have a menu I can look at?" ,

"Yep, let me grab you one," she says, and steps away for a second, "I'll get your drink order in and be back, to give you a minute to look it over."

"Do you want to share an appetizer sampler with me?" Amy asks. "I just need a little something in me if I'm going to drink some more tonight."

"Sure, or order whatever you want; I don't mind."

Our server returns with our drinks, and Amy orders the sampler. "Your order should be out in just a few minutes," she assures us before leaving again.

"So, are you making friends with many of your teammates yet?" Amy asks.

"Yeah, they're a good group of guys. I'm probably closest with Ryker and Jason since they're my linemates, but I've also hung out with Tristan a few times. But really, I'd hang out with anyone from the team," I tell her.

"I was worried about you, coming out here where you didn't know anyone, so I'm glad it's working out so well."

"It isn't like these guys are strangers. I've played against most of them for a few years."

"I get that, but it isn't like you hung out. You chat a few minutes during warmups and chirp at each other during the game."

"You'd be surprised at how much we can say out on the ice." I chuckle.

"I'm sure it's deep conversation." She rolls her eyes at me.

Chuckling, I bring my beer to my lips and take a long pull. "Any big plans for the rest of the year?" I ask.

"I've got Cyndi's bachelorette trip in a few weeks, but other than that, just life as normal."

"Where are you girls going for the weekend?"

"Nashville, and I can't wait! It's going to be so much fun. We rented a house for the weekend and have started planning all the places we want to hit up while we're there. It's going to be epic."

"I can only imagine. Your core group of friends can be kind of crazy, from what I remember, especially when you add in alcohol."

"We're not that bad. No worse than your fraternity was."

"If you say so," I tell her as her food arrives. The smell of the fried food makes what I thought was a full stomach growl.

I reach for a chicken wing, my stomach winning out. "I thought you weren't hungry?" Amy smirks as she bites into a hot mozzarella stick.

"Couldn't resist the smell," I tell her as I bite into the chicken.

"I knew I'd win you over with food. Not much has changed."

"Okay, smart ass."

"You know you love me," Amy says as she takes another bite.

"Always," I tell her. We talk while devouring the platter and our drinks. I decline a refill when the server comes back, as I still have to drive home, and I have a game tomorrow. I try to keep my drinking limited during the season, especially the night before a game. I don't need any hung-over effects hindering my play.

"All right, I should let you get going," Amy says once we've finished eating.

"You're probably right. Thanks again for flying out to go with me tonight."

"Anytime. I'm not usually one to turn down a free mini-vacation or time to see my brother."

"Want me to walk you up to your room?" I offer as we walk out of the bar after I closed out our bill.

"I'm good, you go on home," she insists. I see my sister to the elevator, stopping to pull her into a hug before we part ways.

I head home, exhaustion setting in as I make the drive.

I walk into my condo and drop my keys and wallet on the counter. I grab a water bottle from the fridge and knock it back. The more I can flush the alcohol from my system tonight, the less effect it will have on me tomorrow.

Once in my bedroom, I flip on the TV, which is already on one of the cable sport channels. They're reporting on the game highlights from tonight, before moving on to match-ups tomorrow. They give their opinions on our game before cutting to the interview clip from tonight, as well as showing one of the shots from Amy and I on the red carpet. We clean up nicely, if I do say so myself.

After listening to what they have to say about the Shockwaves and my appearance tonight, I strip out of my suit and head for the shower.

I'm under the hot spray, soaping my body down, doing my best to unwind so I'm ready to sleep once out. My mind wanders back to the thought of Tori the other night, and my cock springs to life.

"Fucking perfect," I mutter to myself. I haven't gotten laid in way too long, and as much as I'd like to change that, I'm not all about the one-night stand. So my left hand will have to suffice another night.

I grip my cock, stroking it a few times as I let my thoughts of Tori wander into dangerous territory. I imagine what her nipples would look like, how they'd taste and respond to the flick of my tongue as I lick them. What her pussy would taste like when my mouth descended upon it and how she'd cry out my name as I made her come time after time. I take my time devouring her and showing her just how much of a lover I am. The idea of her lips wrapped around my shaft has me losing it as I grip my cock tighter and come all over my shower wall.

I rinse my wall off before doing the same to my body and getting out of the shower.

I dry off and wrap the towel around my waist as I step in front of the sink. I brush my teeth, then run a brush through my hair. If I don't, it will be a mess come the morning.

Once in bed, I grab my cell and pull up my message

thread with Tori. It isn't long, just a few texts from the first night we met.

Before I can stop myself, I type out a message and hit send.

Hey, how's it going?

I wait, hoping for a reply, but when one doesn't come in a minute, I drop my phone on the bed next to me and turn my attention back to the TV.

Thirty minutes go by, and still no reply. Maybe she's already asleep for the night, *unless she's out on a date with another guy?* the devil in my mind chimes in.

The idea of her out with someone else just pisses me off, but until she replies, I have no idea.

I plug my phone in and hit the remote to turn the TV off before letting sleep claim me.

I WALK INTO THE ARENA, ANOTHER SUIT FROM MY VAST collection on my body. With the requirement to show up to every game in one, I've collected quite a few over the years. When I was a rookie, I stuck to the cheap ones you can find at practically any department store. The further into my career I got, the more I turned to the designer brands, made with better materials. Now, it's kind of my thing to switch up my suits, some of them flashier than others.

I fist bump the security guards as I pass by. Since I've been here in the arena for a few weeks, I've gotten to know the regular full-time employees, as we see them often.

"Have a good game out there tonight," Shelly, one of the supervisors, tells me as I pass by her.

"Thanks, will do," I tell her as I enter the hallway the dressing and locker rooms are located off of.

I push into the dressing room, finding a couple of other guys in here, as well as one of our equipment guys.

"Aiden, what's up?" Tristan asks as he strips out of his own suit. We use the dressing room as the room we change out of our coming and going clothes and into workout gear or whatever each player prefers to wear while getting ready for the game. For me, it's a team T-shirt, some compression shorts with athletic ones over top.

"Not much, just a chill afternoon, what about you?" I ask as I hang up my suit jacket.

"About the same. I came and worked on my legs this morning to make sure I'm ready for tonight."

"My sister is still in town, and we had kind of a late night last night, so I slept in, then did some yoga before my afternoon nap."

"How did the charity event go?" he asks.

"We had a good time, and they raised a shit ton of money, so I'd say it went well. I definitely dropped some cash last night." I chuckle at the thought of the check I wrote at the end of the night.

"Good for you, man. The next time you get invited to something like that, let me know. I'd like to start giving back to the community."

"Will do. You could also contact the front office. I'm sure they could get you connected with some charity."

"Not a bad idea."

We both focus on getting ready. Every player has his own routine, and we don't usually stray far from those. Superstitions and all that.

"Hey, Cap," I greet Ryker as I join him and some others out in the hallway where we run sprints, or kick around the soccer ball to help loosen us up. "Are your girls coming to the game tonight?"

"Yep, they should be here by puck drop," he says, and a goofy grin covers his face.

"Cap's pussy whipped," Blake Watson, our starting goalie, calls out.

"Watch your mouth," he snaps at him.

"Just calling it like I see it." Blake smirks. "Or would you rather me say she's got you by the balls?"

"She can have them," he fires back. "At least I'm getting laid on a regular basis, it's more than you can say."

"Who says I'm not getting laid?" he questions.

"By the same woman?" Cap asks, quirking a brow at Blake.

"I never said that, but a pussy is a pussy."

"Maybe so, but there's something about committing to just one that hits a little differently," Ryker tells him.

"I've got time until I need to settle down. Don't take my fun away, Cap."

"Just be careful. A new one every night is how you end up with a baby momma, and half your contract gone," he gives his fatherly advice.

"Is that what happened to you?" Blake asks, referring to Ryker's teenage daughter.

"Sort of. Ellie was born right before I hit the NHL, she was only a few months old when I got called up. And her mom wasn't a puck bunny, but Ellie was the product of a fun weekend, one I wouldn't really change. But it's vicious out there, and you don't want to find yourself caught up in a court battle."

"That's why I make sure to wrap it up," Blake insists.

"Condoms fail, trust me. I know from personal experience."

"Time to wrap up the chit-chat and get your asses out on the ice," Coach bellows from the hallway.

We all follow his orders and head for the locker room, where our gear is all waiting in our stalls to get dressed and out on the ice for warmups. I chug down a protein shake from our nutrition staff while I'm getting ready, and head for the ice.

I start out with a few laps around our half of the ice, warming up my legs as the blood flow gets moving. I drop to the ice, stretching out my legs as I look around the arena. Fans have started to fill in, lining up along the glass as they watch everyone come out for warm ups. I see a group of young kids all lined up with signs, hoping a player will toss a puck over the glass to them. One boy in particular is holding a sign saying it's his birthday, so I grab a puck once I'm done stretching and head his way. I tap the glass in front of him, pointing to his sign. "Happy Birthday," I tell him, and toss the puck over the glass to him. The way his face lights up is awesome and I'm glad I could help make his day.

I join my teammates as we start our shooting drills. Ryker passes me the puck and I let it fly off my blade, right into the glove of Blake.

"Better luck next time," he chirps at me as I skate past him.

"I've got your number," I chirp back, and make it my mission to get the puck into the back of his net on my next shot.

Ryker pulls up at the glass, and I notice his daughter, Ellie, and his girlfriend, Avery, are both standing there talking to him. I almost miss her, but behind Avery is Tori. A smile fills my face as I take her in. I jump in the drill once more, but come to a stop at the glass next to Ryker once I'm done, motioning to Tori to step closer.

"Are you avoiding me?" I ask her, as she's still never replied to my text from last night.

Her cheeks redden, and I don't think it's from the coldness of being near the ice. "No," she finally says.

"Then why didn't you text me back?" I ask.

"Just been busy. Sorry."

"I see how it is," I state. "What are you doing after the game?"

"Just heading home, I have to work tomorrow."

"Stick around and have a drink with me after?" I ask.

"Weren't you just out with another woman last night? Did she not put out for you? Is that why you were texting me at midnight?" she snaps, and I'm guessing she saw either the interview or pictures from the event.

"I was out with another woman last night, but she is my sister, so I'd sure hope she wasn't expecting me to take her to bed."

"She was your sister?" she stammers. "You guys look nothing alike. I had no idea."

"Yeah, kind of hard for us to look alike when she was adopted from China as a baby. She flew in for a few days to see me and be my plus one to the event last night. She's actually here tonight, if you wanted to meet her."

"Oh, no, it's okay. I don't want to impose on your time with your family."

"You wouldn't be imposing. Just think about it, please. My sister isn't hanging around after the game tonight since she has an early flight. We can limit it to just one drink," I tell her before I skate away and return to warming up for the game.

CHAPTER 3
TORI

Aiden skates away from me and my chin still feels like it is on the floor. I know what I said to him was on the bitchy side, but how was I supposed to know the bombshell of a woman standing next to him on the red carpet was his sister. As I told him, they look nothing alike, which makes sense, now. When I saw his text message last night, it pissed me off, as I'd just seen his picture online not even an hour beforehand. I assumed the worst and it made me look like the ass that I am.

"What was that all about?" Avery asks once the guys are both gone.

"Just me making an ass out of myself," I tell her, and cover my face in embarrassment.

"How so?" she asks. I'd held off on telling her about Aiden texting me last night until now.

"He texted me last night, but I ignored it and never replied. He called me out on it, and I said something kind of bitchy, and it made me look like an ass."

"What did you say?"

"I asked him if his date refused to put out so that was why he was texting me so late, except, apparently, his date was his sister," I tell her, and her shocked expression shows me all I need to know.

"He has a sister?" she asks.

"Apparently. They look nothing alike because she's adopted. All I know, is the woman on his arm last night was a bombshell, so I assumed it was a romantic date."

"I'd have probably assumed the same thing," Avery assures me. "So what else did he say?"

"He asked me to stick around and go have a drink with him after the game."

"And are you?" she pries.

"I don't know." I chew on a fingernail as I think over her question. "Do you think I should?"

"I think you should do whatever you are comfortable with doing. I've only known Aiden a short amount of time, but in that time, I've come to realize he's a good guy."

"I just don't know. Our chemistry was off the charts the other night, but was it a fluke?"

"Only time can answer the question for you. And actually being around the man."

"Why am I so nervous about going out with him?" I ask.

"Maybe because of the unknown or how strong your connection was. Embarking on a new journey or relationship can be scary, but if we don't take risks in life, we'll miss out on so many amazing things."

"Ugh, why do you have to be so philosophical?"

"Someone has to be the voice of reason," she jokes,

and hits her shoulder against mine as we walk back to our seats.

I get sucked into the game, Ellie answering every question I throw her way as the game plays on in front of us. I'm starting to pick up on things by the second period and get all excited when I turn to her and tell her why the refs blow the whistle on an offsides call against the other team.

"See, you're learning," she praises me. "Before you know it, you'll know as much as I do."

"I think you're giving me a little more credit than I deserve."

"Nah, the more you watch the game, the more you'll pick up."

The final period seems to fly by, mostly in part to the lack of penalty calls tonight. Before I know it, the final buzzer is blasting and the guys all flood the ice as they hug the goalie and celebrate the win on home ice.

"So, what's your verdict? Are you going to go out for a drink?" Avery asks as we wait for the crowd to dissipate.

"I think I am. What's the worst that can happen? We have no chemistry, and we go our separate ways?" I say.

"Exactly, and for all you know, he's your soul mate and you'll fall deeply in love, run off and get married and have all the cute babies to be had."

"I think you're getting a little ahead of yourself." I chuckle at her.

"Just promise me you'll go into things with an open

mind and open heart. Aiden is a good guy. I wouldn't push you his way if I didn't think he was."

I link my pinky with Avery's and tell her, "I promise."

"I'll let you in on a little secret," she says, pulling me in close. "Hockey players have some amazing stamina, use it to your advantage." She smirks.

"Duly noted," I tell her as my mind flashes to what I think Aiden would look like out of his clothes. I'm sure he's well defined underneath his suits, if the way he looks in them has any indication.

"Let's head downstairs so we can wait for the guys in the hallway," Avery suggests.

I follow Ellie and Avery as we make our way back down to the ice level. After flashing our ticket to the security guard, he lets us into the area where we're allowed to wait for the players to come out. I notice Aiden's sister leaning against a wall as she checks something on her phone. I wonder if I should go introduce myself, but chicken out, as it might be a little presumptuous of me to do.

The guys start filing out twenty or so minutes later. All freshly showered and back in their suits. It is a beauty to see them looking so sharp. Aiden and Ryker exit together, and the smile tugging at Aiden's lips when he sees me with Avery and Ellie tells me I made the right decision by sticking around.

He saunters over to me, that smile pulling wider at his lips. "I take it you stuck around for a drink with me tonight?" he asks.

"I'd love to. Is your sister joining us?" I ask him, pointing to where she's still leaning against the wall.

He looks her way and is shocked to see her there. "I don't think so. She originally told me she wasn't sticking around after the game due to her early morning flight."

He walks toward her, but I stay put. I don't want to intrude if something is wrong. He talks to her for a minute or two, before wrapping her in a hug. Once they break apart, they start walking back toward us. My palms start to get sweaty as my nerves kick in. Meeting family members is usually a big step in a relationship, and we're not even in one yet, just going out for drinks together.

"Amy, this is Tori, the woman I was telling you about. Tori, this is my little sister, Amy."

"It's so nice to meet you. I hope he's treating you good. He's been known to be a heart breaker in the past," Amy tells me as we shake hands.

"We've only met just a few days ago, but I can confirm he's been a gentleman since then."

"I'm always a gentleman," he interjects and winks at me, and it does things to me. Things that make my insides clench and butterflies to flitter around in my stomach.

"Good to hear. Maybe he has learned a few manners over the years."

"I'm right here, ladies," he scoffs.

"I'm just giving you shit, and you know it." Amy playfully pats his chest. I'm really enjoying seeing this playful side of Aiden. It somehow makes him feel less intimidating and more relatable.

Amy covers a yawn. "I should go, I've got to be up in a few hours to get to the airport. It was great to meet you. I hope we can get together the next time I visit," Amy says before turning to her brother. "Thanks for the trip out, I had a great time. I love you and I'll let you know I made it home tomorrow when I do."

"Thank you for coming out, I appreciate it and I love you, too. We can walk you out, wait, how were you planning on getting back to the hotel?"

"I was just going to Uber back."

"We can just drop you off, it isn't far away."

"You don't have to do that. I don't want to impose on your evening," she says, trying to push away his offer.

"It isn't a problem," I add. "And then he won't worry you didn't make it back safe," I suggest.

"Okay, fine," Amy gives in.

"Right this way, ladies," Aiden says as he swipes his hand out for us to go ahead of him.

Amy insists I sit up front and she takes the back seat. We drive the few blocks to her hotel and drop her off at the front door.

"Where should we go for our drink?" Aiden asks as he turns my direction.

"It depends, what kind of atmosphere do you want?"

"Someplace intimate and quiet. I'd rather not have to yell over everyone else to talk to you."

"We can go back to my place. I've got some beer and

wine in the fridge." I step way out of my comfort zone with my offer, but it's out there now.

I think I've stunned him, as he is speechless for a solid minute.

"If you're sure," he says. Our moment is interrupted when a car behind us lays on the horn. We are blocking the driveway at the hotel still, so Aiden pulls out so the guy can leave.

"I'm sure, it's just a drink."

"What way do I need to go to head to your place?" he asks, and I direct him.

I lead him inside my building, the walk is silent as so many thoughts run through my mind about how this evening is going to go. I was hesitant on even going to the game tonight with Avery and Ellie, knowing I'd probably see Aiden. I was pissed at him when I thought he'd texted me after going out with another woman, but now realize that jumping to conclusions isn't the smartest thing to do.

"Here we are," I tell him once we reach my door and I slide the key into my lock. I push the door open and flip on the entryway light.

"After you," he states, placing his hand on my door so it stays open while we walk over the threshold. "Nice place," he comments after looking around at the open floor plan.

From the entryway, you can see the kitchen and living room and down the hall where the bedroom and bathroom are. It's small, but perfect for just me.

"Thanks, it works since it's just me. What did you want to drink? Beer or wine?" I ask, needing to do something productive and getting us those drinks will fit the bill.

"I'm good with a beer," Aiden says, but before I can walk away, he pulls me back and spins me around so we're facing one another.

I look up at him, and watch as he takes me in. I can tell he's got something on his mind and wait him out until he speaks again.

"I'm not here to pressure you into anything you don't want, Tori. It's not the kind of man I am. I don't jump from one bed to another. I haven't been intimate with another woman for almost a year."

I gasp at his confession, not sure why I thought he was the opposite. Maybe it was just my idea of what a professional athlete would be.

"From your reaction, I'm guessing you thought differently." He smiles.

"Guilty," I tell him as my cheeks burn in embarrassment. "I'm sorry if I unfairly judged you. Can we start over?" I ask.

"I don't know, I kind of like you all flushed." He smirks. "Gives me an idea of what else would make you all flushed."

Aiden tugs me a little closer, and I can't miss the hardness of his whole body as our fronts press together. His erection presses against my abdomen, which causes my core to clench at the thought of him laying me down and sliding into me. He'd have to stretch me since it's been almost as long for me as he says it's been for him. I push the thought away. It's something for another night, right?

"Can I kiss you, Tori?" Aiden asks, his eyes dropping from mine to my lips and back up again. "I'd really fucking like to kiss you right now."

"Yes," I whisper, giving him permission to do so.

Aiden slides his hands up and cups both sides of my face before he brings his lips to mine in the gentlest kiss I've ever experienced. My eyes slide shut, and I just enjoy the moment. Fireworks explode behind my eye lids as he moves his lips over mine. At the first swipe of his tongue against the seam of my lips, I open for him. He backs me up until I'm pressed against the wall, devouring me as he does so. I can't deny how good it feels to be caged against his rock hard body, and to know I've done this to him. Made him want to devour me.

He tilts my head slightly, tangling his tongue with my own. I can't get enough of him, but the angle my neck is at is becoming a problem. I don't want to, but I break our kiss, pushing him back slightly so my neck isn't angled so high.

"Did I hurt you?" he asks, concern noticeable in his voice.

"I'll be fine, I just couldn't stay like that any longer. Even if the kiss was amazing," I tell him.

"In that case," he says as he sweeps me up in his arms and carries me to the couch. He sits down and places me on his lap before his lips land back on mine.

I'm giddy as we make out on my couch. I realize I have all those warm and fuzzy feelings the movies all show happening when a couple first meets. I've always chalked it up to rom-coms, as I've never experienced this level of butterflies with any other guy from my past.

Aiden is the one to break our kiss, this time. He rests his forehead against mine as he looks deep into my eyes. "What are you doing to me?" he whispers.

"I could ask the same of you," I tell him as I pull away slightly and I sit up straighter. I slide off his lap and onto the couch next to him. I don't miss the way his slacks tent from his erection. "Would you like a beer now?" I offer.

"Nah, but I'll take a water, if you don't mind."

"Of course not," I tell him before jumping up and going to grab us both a glass of water. "Would you like ice?" I ask as I pull two glasses out of the cabinet.

"If it isn't a hassle."

"Not at all," I tell him as I fill both glasses with ice and water from the dispenser in my fridge door. "Here you go," I say as I offer the glass.

"Thank you." He takes the glass from me and pats the cushion next to him, wanting me to sit back down with him.

"When's your next game?" I ask, needing to say something.

"We fly out the day after tomorrow for a road trip, but our first game of the trip isn't until the next day. Since we're going to the East Coast, they try and give us an extra day to deal with the time change. It can wreak havoc on our bodies."

"I can only imagine how hard it is."

"I'm mostly used to it at this point in my career. My rookie season wasn't kind to me. I'd get so fucked up with what time it was with all the travel, I'd get migraines from the lack of sleep. I finally talked to one of the team physicians and they helped me get things regulated so I could sleep when needed and not just lay around for hours. Once I got my sleep under control, I started playing better, which impressed my coach, at the time. He rewarded my efforts with more playing time, which just encouraged me to play that much harder as I saw how it was paying off."

"How old were you when you started playing?" I ask.

"Strapped on my first set of skates when I was three, but started hockey around five."

"I bet you were so cute at that age, out there with all your gear on."

"Are you saying I'm not still cute with all my gear on?" he asks, smirking at me. His smirk quickly turns into a smoldering look, one that could practically melt my panties right off my body.

"Not the way I imagine a five-year-old being cute. But you do look pretty sexy out there on the ice. Especially when you made that little hip check move when you slammed the other guy against the glass," I tell him as I fan my face. "H-O-T," I reiterate as I spell out the word.

"Hot, huh?" he asks as he slips a hand around my neck and pulls me closer to him. He crashes his lips to mine in a searing kiss. "How was that for hot?"

"It will work," I squeak, smiling against his lips.

"I could show you some hip action," he says, his smolder boring into me.

"I'm sure you can," I tell him as I push back. "Maybe another night."

"Okay," he says, and I'm a little shocked he doesn't try and change my answer.

"Just like that?" I ask, a little dumbfounded.

"Yes." He nods his head. "I'm not going to pressure you into anything you don't want or aren't ready for. That's not me."

"Wow," is all I can say. "I can honestly say I've never had that happen. Every man I've been with hasn't stopped so easily when I asked the first time."

"I'm sorry the men in your past have all been assholes; if you give me a chance, I'll show you what a real man is made of."

"I'd like that," I tell him honestly, and those damn butterflies take flight once again.

"I'll start by saying goodnight and letting you get to bed. I know you said you need to be up early for work tomorrow, and I've got an early morning myself," he says as he stands up and takes our glasses back to my kitchen.

It takes a few seconds for everything he's said to register fully and for me to follow him into the kitchen.

"What are you doing tomorrow night?" he asks.

"I don't have any plans, as of now."

"Have dinner with me?" he asks, and wraps his arms around me.

"I suppose I could share a meal with you." I smile up at him and love the way his eyes crinkle as he smiles back at me.

"What time do you get off work and back home?" he asks.

"I should be home by about five thirty or so."

"Can I pick you up at six or do you need more time?" he asks.

"It depends. How dressed up do I need to be?"

"Whatever you're most comfortable in, no dress code for tomorrow night."

"Where is it you're taking me?" I ask, curious since I know he hasn't lived here long, so I'm sure he doesn't know many places yet.

"My place. I'm going to wow you with my grilling skills."

"Well, color me shocked. I wouldn't have guessed you cook for yourself."

"I'm a man of many talents." He winks. "Give me a few days and I'll share more of my hidden talents."

"I'm sure you will," I tell him as he lowers his lips to mine, closing our night out with a kiss just as good as the one we started it out with.

"Good night, Tori. I'll see you tomorrow night," Aiden says before he breaks away from me and walks out my door. I close and lock it after he exits, then turn and lean against it as I slide to the ground in complete shock from the way tonight went. What in the hell just happened? Was it all just a dream or did we really make out multiple times, only for him to kiss me goodnight with a promise for more to come later?

AVERY

Well, how'd the drink date go last
night? Where did y'all go?

I SNEAK A PEEK AT MY PHONE AFTER IT VIBRATED ON MY desk next to me. I've been in back-to-back meetings since I got into the office this morning and it doesn't look like the rest of my day is going to be much different. I'm working with my team on a huge tour for one of our biggest bands.

I'm not presenting at the moment, so I grab my phone to tap out a reply.

{Heart eyes emoji} It was so good. I
can't even put into words what this
man does to me.

We ended up coming back to my
place after dropping his sister off at
her hotel, then talked, made out,
talked some more, made out again
and then he just left when I told him I
wasn't ready for more. Like who does
that?!

See, I told you. Please remember this
and promise me you'll name your first
born after me. {winky face}

Slow your roll there. Definitely not on
the baby train. I've only kissed the man,
but damn can he kiss.

"Tori, what do you think about that idea?" Josh, one of the band's managers asks, and it's the moment I realize I've completely tuned out my meeting as I texted my best friend.

"Sorry, I had to tend to a message, can you repeat the suggestion?" I say into my computer's microphone.

"Sure. We wanted to know what the label thought about having a charity auction for each tour stop, where the winner would get a behind the scenes package. They'll get to attend sound check, have lunch with the band, hang out backstage and see how we get ready for the show. Cap all that off with either suite tickets or front row, whatever is easiest to include."

"I like it. Do you have a charity in mind to support?" I ask, jotting down some ideas of what the package could include.

"What if we picked a local one from each city?" someone suggests.

"I do like the idea. People might be willing to donate more if they knew the money was staying local to their area," I state.

"That would definitely work. We could put out a call for nominations for charities, maybe even select a few to split the money between?"

"It's a possibility. Is this something you'd want to do for every show?" I ask. "It would mean every show day you'd have new fans around all day, unless we switched up the time we do sound check and made it later in the day."

"We can still work out all those details over the coming weeks," Josh offers.

"I agree. How about you work out what the band is willing to add into their daily schedule on show days and get back to me. I don't see why we can't make it happen. I can start to work on finding charities in each city and how we'd run the auction. We'd want the winner selected with notice so they can be prepared for it."

"Sounds like a plan. I'll get back to you next week with what we've come up with, does that work?" Josh asks.

"Works for me," I tell him. "Was there anything else we needed to discuss?" I ask.

"I think we've covered everything on our list," Josh says.

"Great, I'll be in touch next week. Until then, stay out of trouble and enjoy the time off."

I shut the video conference program down and lean back in my office chair. It could have ended so much worse, I think to myself.

I peek at my phone again to see if Avery has messaged me.

So, when are the two of you seeing each other again?

?

Don't ignore me bitch, I need the details.

You'd better have a good excuse on why you're ignoring me all of a sudden.

Okay, text me later. I guess. Love you bitch. {Kissy face emoji}

LOL. Dramatic much? I was in a video conference meeting when you texted earlier and had to jump into the conversation.

To answer your question, we're having dinner tonight. At his house. He's grilling for me apparently.

I'll allow for the reasoning.

Grilling for you, huh? Is that code for rocking your world in bed?

No, but I'm not eliminating sex from the possible outcomes of the evening. From my own research {and by that, I mean all the time he spent pressed against me last night – fully clothed, so there's still some mystery there} he's well equipped. The biggest test is does he know how to use it properly.

I obviously can't vouch for him in the sex department, but remember, hockey players have stamina. Like really fucking good stamina. They play a sixty-minute game, sometimes multiple days in a row. All the time on the ice and in the weight room, builds quite the stamina up. Trust me on that.

I believe you.

Can I ask you a question?

The fact you even need to ask is making me question our friendship.

Feel free to not answer, but was Ryker with anyone recently? Aiden told me it has been almost a year for him and it was kind of hard to believe, but I also don't have any reason not to believe him.

I had the same thought when Ryker and I first got together. Not all professional athletes are man-whores. Some are, but so are everyday average men.

I guess I didn't think of it like that. I hate it's so easy to label them, when in reality it is only a few bad apples who've put the label on athletes.

It really makes you think about not judging a book by the cover, just like you can't judge men by their looks or job.

Quit being so philosophical.

It's one of the reasons you love me so much.

It really is.

I want you to go have the best night with your new man and then once they are gone, we can have a girl's night and talk all about them. Sound good?

Won't you have Ellie when they're gone?

Yeah, but she's cool to hang out with and tends to still stick to her normal nightly routine on the weekends, unless she's hanging out with her best friend.

I could really use a bestie night.

You're mine Friday night. Plan accordingly.

{so excited gif}

Have fun tonight. {winky face} I hope you have trouble walking tomorrow.

Bitch. Don't wish that upon me. I've got boot camp in the morning.

I'm sure the workout Aiden could put you through tonight will suffice as a replacement for tomorrow if you can't walk.

Thanks for making me think of nothing but getting laid tonight.

You're welcome. I think I'll text Aiden now that he owes me something later.

Don't you freaking dare.

I know she's just joking, but my heart does leap into my throat at the idea of her spilling what we've been talking about to him. She'd never break my trust, so I'm good to just relax and push through the rest of my day. The anticipation for tonight builds as each hour slowly ticks by.

CHAPTER 4
AIDEN

I GET HOME FROM THE STORE. I STOPPED AFTER LEAVING practice and grabbed the steaks and shrimp I needed for tonight's dinner. I tend to cook a few nights a week when I'm in town, usually making enough to last me a few meals each time. It makes it easier when cooking for one person, and I don't mind eating the same things a few days in a row.

I get the steaks marinating and back in the fridge so they can soak up the flavors over the next few hours.

I'm just finishing up cleaning the kitchen when my phone rings. I glance at the screen and see Amy's face flashing.

"Make it home okay?" I ask after the video call connects.

"Yep, I'm home and all good. How'd your drinks date go? Tori seemed nice."

"Glad you made it back safely," I tell my sister. "Drinks went good, we're having dinner together tonight." I don't mention we're having said dinner here or that I'm cooking for Tori, as it will lead Amy to jump to conclusions and start thinking I'm on my way to the altar and a happily-ever-after.

"*Eek!* I knew it. The way the two of you looked at each other was," I can hear her kiss her fingertips like she's making the chef's kiss movement, "it was hot, and that's kind of weird to even be saying since you're my brother and all."

"Chill. We're friends that are having dinner together," I stress.

"Mmhmm," Amy hums. "And I'm the Virgin Mary. You are so smitten with Tori, and I'm going to go out on a limb and say she's just as gone for you. The tension between you guys was almost so thick it could have been cut with a knife. And I was only around the two of you for a few minutes, at best."

"Whatever you say," I say to appease my sister.

"You can try and deny it, but you know I'm right. Now, where are you taking her? Please tell me it's somewhere nice."

I was trying not to divulge this quite yet, but I can't bring myself to lie to my sister. "I'm picking her up at six, we're coming back to my place, and I'm cooking. Just picked up some steaks and shrimp. I'll toss together a salad and maybe some pasta for the side."

"Aww, you are so smitten. I hope she realizes just how amazing of a guy you are."

"Thanks for your vote of confidence."

"No, I'm serious. You're a catch. Any woman would be lucky to be with you, and I hope she realizes that."

"You sure know how to stroke a guy's ego." I smirk

to Amy. "How was the flight?" I ask, doing my best to change the subject.

I don't miss Amy's laughter as she allows the subject change. "It was good, easy with the first class ticket and pre-check to get me through security. I didn't check my bag, so I just headed straight to security once I was dropped off at the airport. I breezed through since it was so early in the morning and there was practically no line for pre-check. As soon as I made it through, I placed my Starbucks order in the app and by the time I reached it, my order was waiting for me on the pick-up counter. I grabbed it and went straight to my gate to wait for my flight."

"Sounds smooth enough," I comment.

"Sure was. I can only hope it is easy when I fly to and from Nashville in a few weeks."

"I'm sure it will be fine. Aren't you flying as a group?"

"Yep, so that will be fun. I just hope no one gets drunk before we fly out and causes any problems on the flight. It would be so embarrassing," she says, and I can just imagine how pissed she'd be if someone messed up our trip by doing something stupid on the way to Nashville.

"Hey, I need to do a few things before it's time for me to go pick up Tori, so I'll talk to you later."

"Okay, have a good time. Treat her right," she reminds me.

"Always," I assure her. "The only way to treat a woman is with respect."

"Why can't more guys be like you?" Amy asks, and

I know it's a rhetorical question she doesn't really expect me to answer.

"I'll talk to you in a few days. Don't forget I'm back on the road this week, so if I miss you, it's why."

"I've got your scheduled all programmed into my calendar. I'll try and catch as many of the away games as I can."

"Sounds good. Glad you made it okay. I love you and I'll talk to you soon." I sign off the call with my sister.

I head for my bedroom and change out of the team-issued sweats and T-shirt. Thankfully, the rule about wearing suits to and from the rink is only for games. We don't have anything specific we have to wear when we're going to and from practice. I pull out a pair of dark wash jeans and a solid-colored T-shirt.

Once dressed, I stop in the bathroom and run my electric razor over my few days' long scruff, cutting it back, but not removing it completely.

I head back into the kitchen and start chopping and prepping the side dishes. The more I can get done now, the more time I'll have to spend with Tori and not having to focus on cooking us a fulfilling meal.

I decide to make some potatoes and veggies, so I get them washed, chopped, and into a marinade. I'll grill them right alongside the shrimp and steaks, making things easy on me later. Once I'm done chopping, I add the bowl to the fridge so they can get set up and will be ready for the gill.

I clean the kitchen again, making sure I haven't left a mess anywhere from my prep. I haven't been this nervous about a woman coming over to my place, ever. The knowledge makes me take a step back and think of the significance of what this means. What is it about Tori that has me so tied up in knots? Why am I so enamored by her and want to know everything there is to know about her? We've only just met, yet I feel like I can't get enough time with her.

I find myself daydreaming about the gorgeous and sexy Tori while I wait for the minutes to tick by before I can go pick her up.

Five o'clock finally rolls around and I can't take it any longer, so I grab my keys and wallet from the counter and head for my car. I stop at a flower shop not far away, one I've passed every day on my way to the rink. I check out the options they have made up in their refrigerator cases and settle on one, once I've looked everywhere.

"A beautiful bouquet," the older lady behind the counter comments after I set it down. "Would you like me to wrap it up for you?" she asks.

"Please. Do you also sell a vase it will fit into?" I ask, not sure if I have anything we can put it in.

"Absolutely. Let me grab you a few to choose from in the back." She finishes wrapping the flowers up in paper and then heads into the back room. She returns a minute later with four vase options. They all just look like glass jars to me, so I have no idea what one is best to pick.

"I'll take whatever one you think is best."

"All right. Is this all for you today?" she asks as she starts clicking on her computer.

"The flowers and vase will do it." I pull out my credit card, waiting for the machine to turn green for me to slide my card to pay.

"Thank you for stopping in today," the lady says as I gather the vase and flowers.

"Thanks," I call out before exiting. I place the flowers on the back seat, wondering for a second if I should put the seatbelt around them to keep them from moving around, but decide it's a bit overkill. I'm not going far, and they are just flowers, after all.

I then stop at a little bakery just up the road. I'm not sure how much of a sweet tooth Tori has, but I don't think I can go wrong with having a dessert option on hand.

I enter the little shop and make my way to the display case. It is filled with so many options, all miniature in size.

"Welcome to Sweet Delights, how can I help you today?" the young girl behind the counter asks.

"I just need some dessert for a dinner tonight."

"You've come to the right place then; do you have an idea of what you'd like to serve?" she asks.

"No clue, but seeing as how everything is already miniature, maybe a box with a few options will work."

"We have a six-option box. Would you like to go with it?"

"That'll be perfect," I tell her, and proceed to let her pick the six items, only asking they all be different, so we have a good selection to choose from later tonight.

Since I've got time to kill still, I run back home to drop the flowers and dessert off.

I arrive at Tori's condo ten minutes early. Even with my two stops, and running home, I'm still early. I sit here for a minute, trying to kill the time, but my desire to get my eyes and lips on her wins out and I head inside the building. Another resident is leaving and lets me in the secure door, thus bypassing the need to call her to be let in.

I quickly make my way to her door, rapping my knuckles on the frame.

The door swings open, and the most gorgeous woman stands in front of me. "Oh, hi," she greets, "I wasn't expecting you already. I thought it was one of my neighbors bringing me mail or asking to borrow something. How'd you get in?"

"Hi. Someone was leaving as I was arriving, and they let me in. Makes your secure entrance not so secure."

"Yeah, it can become a problem, but I'm just as guilty. Don't really want to be the asshole who doesn't let someone in when you're there at the door."

"It wouldn't make you an asshole. You're keeping yourself safe by not allowing someone you don't know in."

"Speaking of letting someone in, would you like to come in?" Tori asks. She steps back, opening the door wider and giving me the room to walk in.

I step inside and give her space to close the door behind us. As soon as the latch clicks shut, I pull her into my arms and press my lips to hers. "I've been thinking about kissing you all day," I admit against her lips.

"I might be guilty of the same thing," she confesses, and smiles up at me.

"Are you ready to go?" I ask as we step apart from one another.

"Yep, let me just grab my things and we can head out."

I stay near the door as she scurries away to grab whatever it is she needs and shut lights off as she returns.

"Ready?" I ask as I reach for the door handle.

"Yep, but I was thinking, wouldn't it be easier if I just followed you to your place? Then, you won't have to drive me back at the end of the night."

"I don't mind," I tell her as I lean in and kiss her cheek. "It will give me a few more minutes with you."

"Aww, you want to spend more time with me; so sweet of you."

"I'd spend every second you give me with you," I tell her before opening the door for the two of us. We stop once outside the door so she can lock it.

I slip my hand into hers, and we proceed to my car. I unlock the doors as we approach and open the passenger door for her once we reach it. "Thank you," she says before letting go of my hand and sliding into the seat.

I make sure she's inside before closing the door, then rounding the back of the car so I can get into the driver's side.

"So, what are you dazzling me with for dinner tonight?" Tori asks once we're out on the road.

"Grilled steak and shrimp, with some grilled

veggies on the side. I stopped at a little bakery and picked up a box of miniature desserts for us to choose from."

"Wow, you aren't skimping on anything, are you?" she muses as I take the exit for my condo.

"A man's got to eat, and I know the importance of dessert after a good meal." I wink at her as I pull into my garage.

"Wow, what a view," Tori gasps after I lead her inside my condo. It sits up pretty high in the building and has an amazing view of the San Francisco skyline. On clear nights like tonight, I can see all the boats and ships dotting the water. I enjoy sitting out on my balcony and watching them all float by. Even with the hustle and bustle of the city below, watching them from this height is calming, somehow.

"One of the selling points when I signed my lease."

"I bet. Do you just rent here, then?" she asks.

"Yeah, I wasn't sure where I'd want to buy a house, or if I even do. Playing professional sports is still a business and at the end of the day, I could be traded. Renting is sometimes easier, especially for the first year or so. It will give me time to learn the city some and really think about if I want to buy here or just keep renting."

"I can see that. Do you own a home anywhere else?" she asks.

"I do. I have one back in Minnesota, where I'm from. It's on a lake and is where I spend most of my off time."

"Is it where your sister and other family lives?"

"Amy lives in the city, so she's about an hour away.

My parents are about a half hour or so away. They still live in my childhood home," I tell her.

"So sweet. How long have they been married?"

"They celebrate their thirtieth anniversary next year. Amy wants to throw them a big party to celebrate."

"Wow! What a milestone to celebrate. One I can only hope to hit one day, myself."

"You want to get married and have kids?" I ask, curious to her answer.

"Yeah. I know my job isn't very family-friendly, but I hope to make it work, one day. I've been saving since I started working and have a nest egg saved up. It would be nice to get married and once we're ready for kids, quit my job to stay home, at least for the first few years, when they're little. I probably won't be able to live here in the city and make it happen, but I'm okay with that. Moving doesn't sound horrible."

"Did you grow up here?" I ask as I head for the balcony.

"No, my family is from Idaho. I came out for college, loved it so much and, then scored an internship during my junior year with the record label. My internship led to a job offer and I've never looked back."

"Wow, Idaho to California. That's a bit different way of life." I uncover the grill and get it fired up to start pre-heating.

"It really is, but I made some amazing friends in college, and it slowly became home to me. By the time I graduated college, I didn't want to leave, even though it is so expensive to live here. Avery and I lived together for a few years, as neither of us could afford a place on our own. Once we could, we both decided we wanted some more independence, and both moved. It was hard, at first, but we both got used to it. My parents now have a place down here they like to winter at, so I see them more during the cold months of the year. Do you need help with anything?" Tori offers as I head back inside to grab the food to start grilling.

"I'm all set, but can I get you something to drink?" I ask as I make my way back into the kitchen. I notice the flowers on the counter and realize I never gave them to Tori. "Shit, I forgot to give these to you," I tell her as I hold them up.

"These are beautiful," she says, walking over to join me in the kitchen. I grab the vase I bought and fill it halfway with some water.

"Not as beautiful as you are," I tell her as I lean over and kiss her cheek. I set the vase on the counter and reach for the flowers.

"No need to sweet talk me, I'm already here with you tonight." She smirks but keeps the flowers in her hands. "I've got these, you work on the food."

I watch as she unravels the twine and paper the florist packaged them up with. "Do you have any scissors?" Tori asks once she has them unpackaged.

"Yeah, in the center of the knife block," I say and motion to where it sits next to the stovetop. "What do you need to cut? Hopefully not me?"

Tori lets out a little laugh as she reaches for the scissors. "Definitely not you." She flashes a smile my way. "Just the ends of the stems. It helps them to last longer; they can absorb more water and nutrients with freshly cut stems. If you put them in without cutting, they've already sealed off from where they were previously cut and won't soak up the water."

"Wow, I never knew all that," I admit.

"If cutting the stems blows your mind, this will really shock you. Do you have any white vinegar or bleach and some sugar?" she asks.

"I think so. Check in the cabinet above the stove for vinegar, and the sugar is in a canister in the small spice cabinet," I tell her as I place the marinated steaks and shrimp out on a platter so I can carry them out to the grill. "What is vinegar and sugar going to do?" I ask as she finds the bottle of vinegar.

"The sugar will nourish the flowers and trigger them to bloom, the vinegar will keep bacteria from growing and keep the blooms fresher, longer."

"Interesting, I guess you learn something new every day."

"My mom loves flowers, and she grows a huge garden every year. As soon as they start to bloom, she's cutting them to bring inside and display on the table. Once winter rolls around and she doesn't have any to bring inside, my dad brings her a bouquet every week like clockwork."

"Ah, so he's a romantic guy."

"You could say that," she agrees. "I've watched the two of them fall deeper and deeper in love with each other my entire life. I can only hope to find someone to love me a tenth of the amount they love and respect each other."

"Only a tenth, why not one hundred?" I ask. From

the little I've known Tori, I think she deserves the world, and it includes a man who thinks she's his entire world.

"Because a love like they have is one-in-a-million. I'm not sure it could ever be replicated."

"Maybe not their exact love, but my guess is yours will be just as special." I lean over and kiss her cheek before heading back out to the grill with the platter of food. I open the lid and the heat hits me in the face. I scrape off the grates before placing the food down on it. The steaks sizzle, and I know they'll come out with a nice sear on them. I add the grill basket filled with shrimp and the basket with the potatoes and veggies before I close the lid and let them all do their thing.

"Did you want something to drink?" I ask when I enter again. I realize we got sidetracked by the flowers and I never followed up with Tori.

"Sure, what are my options?" she asks as she finishes arranging the flowers in the vase.

"I've got," I start to say as I make my way to the fridge and open it up. "Water, juice, milk, beer, wine, or I can shake up some margaritas or something from the bar cart," I offer up, pointing to my dining room where I have a fully loaded bar area.

"I'm fine with a glass of wine."

I pull down two glasses and grab the bottle already chilled in the fridge. "Is this one okay?" I ask, showing her the bottle of Pinot Noir.

"It's perfect," Tori says after looking over the label. "Fancy, fancy. Are you trying to impress me, Mr. Fox?" she purrs as I hand over her glass.

"If a bottle of wine will impress you, then sure thing, Ms. Ferguson." I smirk and pull her into me.

"Only one of the ways you can impress me, Mr. Fox," Tori says as she presses her body against mine. I don't miss the way her eyes drop down as she does so. My dick twitches in my jeans as she presses into me.

"Oh, Ms. Ferguson, I've got more ways to impress you. A hard one, right here, if you're so inclined to test it out after dinner."

I kiss her, stealing her breath and any words she was going to reply with. I slide a hand up her back, not stopping until I cup the back of her neck, turning her just so to give me better access to deepen the kiss.

The timer on my watch starts to vibrate, letting me know it is time to flip the steaks. I break our connection, resting my forehead against hers. "The grill is calling," I tell her, pre-answering the question I can see in her eyes as to why I stopped.

Tori follows me out onto the deck and takes a seat in one of the loungers. Her glass of wine pressed to her lips as she watches me flip the food. I have to take my eyes off of her so I don't burn myself, but make quick work of flipping and checking on everything.

I close the lid of the grill and make my way across the deck to the lounger. "Join me," Tori states, patting the chair where she'd like me to sit down. I'm not going to waste an invitation like that, so I sit down and lean back. "How long until dinner is ready?" she asks.

"How do you like your steak cooked? I realized I should have asked you already."

"Medium is great," she says.

"Perfect. They should be done in about eight minutes."

"Can I help you get the table ready?" she offers.

"Sure, but before we do, I need to kiss you again," I tell her as I pull her back to me, resuming the kiss we'd shared before my alarm went off.

CHAPTER 5
TORI

Aiden cups my cheeks as his tongue duels with my own. The way this man can take complete control of my body in a matter of seconds is a new experience. I've been with a handful of guys in my past, but none make me feel like this one does. The way it feels like he's cherishing every touch, every moment we're together, like he needs to memorize them all.

I felt his watch vibrate again, alerting him it's time to tend to the grill. My stomach takes that moment to let out a loud noise as my hunger wins out on importance.

Aiden chuckles against my lips. "Hungry?" he asks.

"Starving, actually; I didn't have time today for a full lunch."

"Then let's get you fed; good thing I made extras."

I stand up from the chair, allowing him to do the same after we'd become tangled up together. I can't get enough of his natural swagger. The confidence this man has is intoxicating and sexy. His muscles flex as he opens the grill's lid and removes the food onto a clean platter.

"Did you want to eat outside or inside?" he asks.

"I'm fine with either; it's pleasant out here if you want to just stay outside," I tell him.

He carries the platter to his outdoor table, setting it down in the center. The food looks and smells amazing. As the smell hits my senses, my stomach lets out another cry of hunger.

"I'll go grab us some plates and utensils. Do you need a refill on your wine?" Aiden asks.

"I'm good on the wine, but I'd take a glass of water. Do you need any help getting everything out here?" I offer.

"That'd be great, thank you," he replies and holds out a hand for me to go in front of him through the door. I head straight for the kitchen and open the cabinet he took the wine glass from, finding some water glasses on the bottom shelf.

"Do you want a glass of water?" I ask as I reached for a glass.

"Yes, please," he says and leans over and kisses my cheek as he grabs silverware from the drawer.

It's kind of crazy how easily we both slip into this domestic mode of getting ready for dinner together. It's like we've done this many times, yet it is our first time. With two glasses filled with ice water, I follow Aiden back outside. His hands are full of plates, silverware, napkins, and salt and pepper shakers.

We make quick work of setting the table, and his gentlemanly side definitely comes out as he pulls a chair out for me to sit down in, helping me scoot it in after I take a seat.

"This looks amazing, better than I could ever do," I tell him as I fill my plate with all the amazing food he just cooked.

"Thank you; I've gotten used to cooking healthy for myself over the years. I usually grill up a bunch every few days, portion it out, and have home-cooked meals ready to reheat each day I'm home. It keeps me from ordering too much takeout or stopping all the time on my way home."

"Very smart; I'm guilty of ordering takeout way too much. Cooking for one isn't fun or easy all that often. And I'm not the greatest with leftovers."

"I was the same way, at first, but I realized just how much of a disservice I was doing to my body by not eating healthy enough. I expect a lot out of my body, and I need to fuel it correctly."

I can't help myself as my eyes drag up and down his body. I can only see the side of him, the way we're seated at the table, but I've gotten a good look at him while he's been standing, or hell, while I've straddled his lap. The man is not lacking in the muscle department. *At all.*

"Like something you see?" He smirks.

"You are definitely easy on the eyes," I reply.

"Just wait until you see me naked." He winks, and I toss my head back in a fit of laughter. "Is the thought of seeing me naked funny?" he asks, his tone a little serious.

"God no, and I'm sorry if that was offensive. I was laughing at your cockiness," I apologize quickly.

"I'm just giving you shit, Tori. I didn't take offense."

I smack my chest with my hand. "You just about gave me a heart attack."

He smirks again. "Sorry," he says, shrugging his shoulders as if he isn't sorry one bit.

The next forty-five minutes or so goes by in the blink of an eye. We talk, bantering back and forth as we crack each other up with funny stories or one-liners. It feels so good to be here with him, like this, as we get to know one another. Feeling out this mutual attraction we both appear to have with one another.

Once we're done eating, we work together to clean up the table and fill the dishwasher with our dirty dishes.

"Are you ready for some dessert or do you need a little bit?" Aiden asks once the kitchen is cleaned up.

"I need a little longer before I can eat anything else. I'm still stuffed, but it was so good," I tell him.

"It was damn good, if I do say so myself," he boasts a little bit. He links our fingers together and tugs me to follow him. I'd probably follow this man anywhere he wanted to take me at this moment, so I'm a little shocked when he leads me to the couch. I was somewhat expecting him to try and lead me to his bedroom, but he doesn't. "Sit," he instructs, tugging my hand to sit down next to him.

I do as asked and sit down next to him. However, I don't sit the same way he is; I turn so I'm sideways on the couch, allowing me to face him.

Aiden caresses my face, his thumb trailing over my bottom lip. I flick my tongue out, wetting the pad of his thumb in the process. His eyes flair, darkening in the process. "Fucking vixen," he hisses, and I do it again, this time sucking the tip of his thumb between my lips. My eyes drop down as the bulge in his jeans grows. I flick the tip of his thumb and swear I see his cock twitch in reply. "You're going to kill me, woman." His deep, gravely voice goes straight to my clit.

I release the tip of his thumb. "No killing, just teasing." I smile at him and flutter my lashes.

"Yep, you're going to kill me, woman." He groans but pulls me into his lap.

I beat him to the punch and press my lips to his. He's intoxicating, and I can't get enough, which scares me slightly. Not enough to stop, but fear does linger in the back of my mind.

Aiden slips his fingers beneath my top; I'd changed into my favorite skinny jeans and a flowing top after getting home from work. As his rough fingers skim across my skin, goose bumps break out in his wake. "So fucking soft," he murmurs. His hands hardly touch me, yet I feel on fire from his simple touch as he caresses my back and sides.

I explore his chest with my own hands, greedy as I try and take him all in. However, it isn't as easy since I can't feel his skin with his shirt between us.

"I need more of you," he says after breaking the kiss and moving his lips along my jaw and down my neck.

"I need more of you," I tell him as I tug at his shirt. Just as quickly as we came together, he stands with me in his arms and starts walking down the hall toward the bedroom door.

Once we're inside his bedroom, he sets me down but doesn't let go. We're facing one another; Aiden's hands are on my hips as he holds me close. With our bodies this close to each other, I have to tip my head back to look up at him completely. I'm not a short woman, but he's well over six feet tall, so he engulfs my five-foot-ten-inch body. I can tell by the way he looks down at me he's contemplating something; what that is, I have no clue.

"Everything okay?" I finally ask, finding my voice.

"Just soaking everything in, and I wanted to give you a minute to decide if this is too much too soon. The last thing I want to do is pressure you into something you don't want or aren't ready for. I enjoy spending time with you and don't want to fuck it up by rushing anything."

I reach up and cup his face. I love the way his scruff feels against my hand. I have to rub my thighs together as the thought of what it would feel like *there* flashes in my mind. "I'm right where I want to be," I assure him, and push up on my toes so I can kiss him gently.

That must have been the assurance he needed because before I know what is even happening, he bends down and picks me straight up off the floor, carrying me a few feet to his bed. He gently sets me down, my ass hitting the mattress, and my body falls backward, Aiden coming with me, never breaking our kiss.

We make out for a few more minutes before he

pushes away, standing at the edge of the bed and between my legs. He reaches behind his neck and tugs twice before his polo releases from his pants and pulls up his body. He tugs it over his head and tosses it to the side. This is the first time I'm seeing his sinewy chest, and damn if it doesn't make my mouth water.

I sit up and run my hands over the exposed skin, his muscles twitching in my wake. "I think you're over-dressed," he says.

I lift my arms up, giving him the go-ahead to pull my shirt off over my head, and he doesn't miss a beat, reaching down to grab the hem and pulling it up. "So beautiful," Aiden whispers as he drops my shirt off the end of the bed. He returns his hands to my body, trailing his fingers along the top of my bra. My nipples harden underneath the smooth material as he edges closer to them.

Aiden drops to his knees, his body still neatly settled between my legs. He tugs down the cup on my left breast and groans at the sight of my hardened peak. His thumb flicks over the tight bud a few times before his mouth descends, sucking and lapping at my nipple. "So sweet," he states against my skin. He reaches behind me and finds the clasp of my bra, easily opening it with one twist of his wrist.

The straps fall from my shoulders, then from the front of my body. Aiden plucks the material and tosses it out of the way, sending it to join our shirts on the floor. He cups both of my breasts, filling each palm with a nice handful. "Enjoying yourself?" I ask as I watch him switch back and forth between sides. His eyes flick up to mine, and the desire I see in them almost sets me on fire.

"Immensely," he says. "I'm not just saying this because we're here right now, or because I'm trying to get some brownie points, but you have the most amazing tits I've ever seen," he says before dropping open mouth kisses to the swells of my breasts. "Or tasted." He flicks the tip of his tongue across my stiff nipples.

"Ah," I cry out, my body strung so tight, and he's only fondled my breasts, at this point.

"You like that?" he asks, and does it again.

"Yeah," I pant, and slide my hands into his hair, tugging him closer and holding him against my body so he won't stop his assault on my breasts.

"Lie back," he instructs as he presses against my breastbone. I do as asked and fall back on the bed. He stands, and I take the opportunity to push my body up the bed further. "Can we lose these?" he asks, tugging at the hem of my jeans.

"That depends." I smile at him.

"On what?" He plays along.

"Mine can come off if yours also come off," I tell him.

He doesn't even answer, just reaches down and undoes his shorts. They fall from his perfectly chiseled body, and I'm speechless when I get my first look at all he has to offer, or at least what I can tell from the tightness of his boxer briefs still covering the family jewels. "Once again, I'm feeling like you're overdressed." He smirks down at me.

"Funny." I laugh and pat his chest before reaching down and unbuttoning my jeans. Aiden knocks my hands away, taking over and lowering the zipper before tugging them down my hips. I lift my ass off the bed, giving him a little clearance to do so. He leaves my panties in place, I'm not sure yet if that was on purpose because he wants the barrier between us still or because he wants me to give him permission. Either way, I'm fine making out with him just like this.

Once my jeans are out of the way, Aiden hovers over me. His eyes bore into my own as we take one another in. All I can hear is the whooshing of my heartbeat in my ears as the rate increases in anticipation of what's next, what move he'll make, and where he'll kiss or touch me.

"You ready for more?" he asks, and lowers his body down; his lips find the sensitive area where my neck meets my shoulder.

I hum my agreement and greedily pull his body closer to my own. I love the feel of his body pressed against mine. He kisses his way down, switching from open-mouth kisses to little nips of my skin. The anticipation of what he'll do next has my body humming and alive.

He sucks one breast into his mouth, playing with my other one simultaneously. He rolls my nipples, flicking and plucking at them as he drives me wild before abruptly releasing my breast with a pop and lowering even further down the bed.

Aiden nips at the tender flesh on the underside of my breasts, immediately running his tongue across the skin to soothe the sting he's created. "Your body comes alive so easily," he says between kisses to my abdomen.

"Just for you," I tell him as I try and focus on his every move. My panties are soaked as my clit pulses with need. A need I hope he's about to fulfill. If not, my bob will definitely be getting a workout tonight.

"Is that so?" he asks as he slides further down. He picks up one of my legs and tosses it over his shoulder, repeating the motion with my other one. "How reactive are you here?" he asks, and slides his fingers overtop my panties, from my clit to my opening.

"Fuck," I cry out, the buildup too intense. He doesn't require any further words, which is good because I don't think I could form a coherent sentence right now. Not with his mouth so close to my center.

Aiden tucks his fingers into the elastic band of my panties and tugs. I lift my ass off the bed by an inch or so, and he easily pulls them off. He rolls to the side, giving himself the room needed to pull them completely off my legs. I hardly notice them go flying somewhere off the bed. He settles back on the bed, my legs back in place over his shoulders. He circles my clit with a finger as he opens up my most private areas to him.

"So fucking perfect," he states before descending on me. His tongue laps from my opening up to my clit in what has to be the fastest lick ever. He replaces the circling of my clit with his tongue before sucking on it hard. My back arches off the bed, but his strong arm comes up and holds me still, pinning me to the mattress as he goes to town on my clit. It doesn't take long before

I'm seeing my first set of stars of the night. "Good girl," he says against my skin as I stop shaking. "Now, do it again," he instructs, and slides two fingers inside me. He's relentless, searching out another orgasm with only his mouth and fingers doing all the work.

"I don't know if I can come again," I pant out, my body edging closer to another orgasm.

"You can. Now, be a good girl and come on my fingers," he demands. I've never had a man talk to me like this, but it must be a new kink level unlocked and my body responds as the orgasm barrels out of me. I didn't even realize I was so close to the edge, but I go soaring over it. My body is rigid, then completely limp as I bask in the goodness of my orgasm.

"Good girl," Aiden praises as he pushes up the bed, leaving soft kisses in his wake.

I have no idea how long I lay there with my eyes closed, recuperating from my two orgasms. Probably the two most intense orgasms I've had in my entire life. "Hi," I whisper as I turn my head his way and peek my eyes open.

"Feeling good?" he asks as he rubs a hand along my side. The movement of his skin on mine sends tingles down my body and goose bumps along my skin.

"So good, like, incredibly good," I tell him. "I don't think I've ever felt this relaxed or cherished."

"I can work with incredible," he presses his lips to mine, "but let's try and make it magnificent, or whatever word is better than incredible."

"I'm not sure that's possible," I tell him as he rolls over and opens his nightstand drawer. He pulls out a condom, and I watch as he shucks his boxer briefs, first, before opening the packet, then rolling the condom down his shaft.

"It's possible; trust me on this one." He smirks.

"You're pretty confident," I state.

"I am. Just enjoy the feeling," Aiden instructs as he settles himself back between my legs. He teases my entrance with his tip, sliding it up and over my clit before bringing it back down and pressing it inside me.

I gasp as he slides in, the fullness of his cock as it stretches me to accommodate his size. "So tight," I manage to say.

"Just breathe," he instructs, and I do as told. "Such a good girl, taking my cock all the way."

"I need—" I start to say, but can't finish my sentence as I can no longer form words as he slides out and slams back into me. The sensations taking over my entire body are unlike anything else I've experienced.

Aiden takes complete control, and I gladly give him all of it. His rhythm is fast, our bodies slapping together every few seconds as his hips piston back and forth. He slows, but doesn't come to a complete stop, moving my legs until my feet are propped up on his shoulders. He presses down, kissing me hard as he starts to pump faster. The new angle is everything and I can feel my body tighten as it's ready to explode yet again.

"Aiden," I cry out seconds later, just as his cock hits my g-spot and sends me flying over the edge. I can feel the wetness from my orgasm leaking out of me as he keeps his thrusts consistent.

"That's my good girl," he praises between kissing

my cheek. "I'm going to fill you up now, are you ready?" he asks.

All I can do is nod in agreement. I still can't really form words at the moment; my mind is still too scrambled from the multiple orgasms he's provided tonight.

Aiden speeds up slightly, and I can tell he's on the cusp of his own orgasm. I feel his cock swell, my walls contracting around his size. He thrusts hard, holding his hips pressed to mine as his orgasm takes hold, barreling out of him and filling the condom. "Fuck," he bellows.

I don't think I've experienced a guy's orgasm lasting as long as this, but it's truly an experience. One I can only hope isn't a one-time thing.

Aiden opens his eyes, looking down at me below him. "Are you okay?" he asks, and drops a chaste kiss on my lips.

"Perfect," I tell him as I run my fingers through his sweaty hair.

He kisses me again before pulling out and sliding off the bed to go take care of the condom. He returns from the bathroom with a wet washcloth in his hands. "Open for me," Aiden says, and I do as he asks. I'm touched by his kindness and willingness to take care of me. He wipes my inner thighs, then along my center. "We can get the rest in the shower." He winks before tossing the washcloth toward the bathroom door and sliding into bed next to me.

"Thank you," I say as we both move toward one another. I'm not sure if it's a subconscious thing or what, but we end up on our sides, facing one another with our faces only inches apart. Aiden has his legs tangled with mine and his hand on my hip. His fingers trace designs on my bare skin, causing me to squirm slightly under his touch.

"Are you ticklish?" he asks as a grin tugs at his lips.

"Maybe," I say, doing my best to hold it together. The sensation takes over, and I laugh and squirm, trying to get away from the ticklish feeling. All it does is bring our bodies closer, flush against one another.

"How's this?" he asks, and rubs his stubble along my neck. I'm going to have beard burn if he keeps this up. Hell, I probably already do on my thighs from the amount of time I spent riding his face earlier.

"Good." I moan as he sucks along the sensitive skin. "How are you already hard again?" I ask as I feel his erection pressing against my belly.

"It's all you," he says into my skin. "Just one look at you, and I'm hard. Heaven help me, now that you're naked and pressed up against me in bed. I don't think I'll ever go soft in this position."

"You might have the stamina of a professional athlete, but I sure as hell don't."

"Just because I'm hard doesn't mean I expect sex from you. I quite enjoy making you squirm," he says before doing just that again.

CHAPTER 6
AIDEN

THE CONTENTMENT I'M FEELING WITH TORI IN MY ARMS IS one I can't say I've felt before. I don't think it is the butterflies that come with a new relationship. I think this is genuinely something special between the two of us. Like, I've found my true soulmate.

"Are you ready for dessert?" I ask. We've been lying here for probably an hour. Alternating between kissing and talking. Just getting to know one another on a deeper level.

"I could be talked into something sweet," she says.

"Then stay right here; I'll be back," I state, and pop out of bed. I snag my boxer briefs off the floor and pull them on. My cock is still at half-mast, mainly because I've been lying in bed with a beautiful woman in my arms. "Do you need anything else while I'm up?" I ask before walking out the bedroom door.

"Maybe something to drink?" She smiles at me and tugs the sheet over her body.

I take one last look at her sprawled out in my bed—

a look I could easily get used to—before I turn and head down the hall and into the kitchen. I refill our water glasses from dinner and grab the container from the fridge holding the desserts I picked up. I transfer them to a plate and select two forks from the drawer before heading back down the hall. I've got everything balanced, so I set the glasses down on the nightstand before handing over the plate with six mini dessert options all laid out on it.

"Mhmm, these look delicious," Tori says as she licks her lips.

"You look delicious," I tell her, unable to let the opening go.

"If you play your cards right, maybe I'll let you have another taste tonight." She winks up at me before taking one of the forks and sliding it into the salted caramel cheesecake. I watch intently as she glides the fork into her mouth, her lips wrapping around the metal. I swear I can feel her lips wrapping around my cock in the moment. The same moment I go from half hard to fully hard. The tip of my cock pushes out the top of my briefs, and there's not a damn thing I can do about it. "Mhmmm, this is so damn good," Tori says as she pulls the fork from her mouth. Her eyes roll shut, and her head connects with my headboard.

"Orgasmic good?" I ask, reaching for the plate so she doesn't drop it with her eyes closed.

"Possibly," she says, a smile tugging at her lips as she opens her eyes back up and they find mine. "But nowhere near as good as the orgasms you give me."

"Good to know I'm better than some sugar and

cream." I smirk and take a bite of my own. It is good, great, really, so I can see why she'd say what she did about it. I try the next item on the plate, this one a raspberry lemon cake. "Try this one," I say, offering her a bite. Her eyes find mine again and we don't break contact as I slide the fork between her lips, and she takes the food from it. The tension is crackling between us, one right move and we'll combust. Who would have thought eating dessert could be such a turn on.

We manage to at least try all six options on the plate before we set it aside. I swipe some of the frosting off of the raspberry lemon cake and then over her nipple. "Oops." I smirk, lowering my mouth to her breasts as I clean them off.

"You're incorrigible." Tori laughs as I kiss my way lower.

"Only with you," I tell her as I circle her clit with my tongue.

"Aiden," she cries out, "I can't."

"Oh, sweetheart, you can. Just be a good girl and let your body relax. Let me make you feel like you've never felt before," I coach, and then feel her relax underneath me.

Her sweetness hits my tongue, and I know she's all mine. I have her just where I want her and could easily keep her here all night long, racking her body with as much pleasure as I can possibly create.

"That's it, baby," I whisper into her skin as her body shakes. I slide two fingers inside her, finding her perfect spot I've quickly learned will set her off instantly. I suck her clit hard as I rub the inside. Her body arches off the bed as my name falls from her lips in the most beautiful way I've heard it called out.

I ROLL OVER AND COME INTO CONTACT WITH A WARM BODY. It takes my brain a couple of seconds to recount where I'm at and who's in bed next to me. The memories of the previous few hours all come back, the multiple orgasms, the dessert, the subsequent fucking that took place. I'm exhausted but in the best way possible.

I slip an arm around Tori, pulling her warm body into my own. She's peacefully sleeping, and her calm breathing quickly lulls me back to sleep for a few more hours.

"SHIT, SHIT SHIT!" I STARTLE AWAKE, TORI FRANTICALLY moving about my room as she picks up our clothes from last night.

"Everything okay?" I ask as I push up to a sitting position. My voice is groggy with sleep.

"No, I'm late and need to get to work. I've got a big meeting this morning," she says as she hops around, trying to step into her panties. The same ones I peeled off her body with my teeth around three a.m. for the last time.

"Okay, just take a deep breath. I'll take you straight there. You can go take a quick shower and I'll make you some breakfast to take in the car, how's that sound?" I offer.

"I don't have anything with me to shower with or clean clothes, and I can't show up in skinny jeans and this top." She gives me a wild look, like my suggestion is crazy.

"Okay, then, let's go, I'll make you breakfast at your place while you shower there."

"I'm so fucked," she says under her breath.

I hop from the bed, naked as the day I was born. I make my way to where she's standing, now clasping her bra as she works toward getting dressed.

"Try and take a few deep breaths. Everything will work out the way it's supposed to."

"I can't believe I fell asleep here; I knew I should have told you no after dessert," she says, poking my chest like this is all my fault.

"What can I say? I've got a magical cock; one I'm pretty sure you enjoyed a lot of last night." I smirk.

"Not helping!" she cries out and picks up her jeans.

I watch as she pulls them on, then grabs her shirt and turns it right side out before slipping it over her head. "Are you going to put some clothes on or just stand there naked all day?"

"I don't know, I think you like looking at me naked." I smile but quickly realize this isn't the time to joke with her.

"Please, Aiden. I really need to go. This is serious and not the time to play games or joke."

I walk to my dresser and pull out a T-shirt and

shorts, putting both on quickly. I slip on some slides and am ready to walk out the door.

"Let's go," I instruct. I grab my cell, keys, and wallet, and we're out the door. Tori follows closely behind me. I can feel the stress rolling off of her in waves.

I open the passenger door for her to slide in. Her facial features are pulled into a tight line, almost passing for some resting bitch face, but I know it's just the stress of being late that is getting to her.

I pull out onto the highway, thankful the traffic doesn't appear to be heavy this morning. "What can I do to help you this morning?" I ask as I pull off the highway at her exit.

"Nothing, just drop me off, and I'll be good to go from there," she says, but keeps looking out the window away from me.

"Tori, I'm sorry you are late and that I let you fall asleep at my place. It wasn't my intention to make your morning a bad one. Let me help you; it's the least I can do."

"I'm not mad at you, just stressed. I'm never late; this is very unlike me."

"Then your work should be understanding. Everyone has an off day or oversleeps every once in a while. Give yourself some grace; you're only human, after all."

"I sent my team a text letting them know I'd be late. I should have enough time to shower and get ready and then into the office before our meeting starts, I just won't be able to meet with my team for our pre-meeting meeting."

"A pre-meeting meeting?" I question, because it just sounds horrible.

Tori chuckles, and the sound gives me a slice of hope she'll relax about our morning. "Whenever we have large meetings with our talent, I always like to meet with my team one last time to go over everything we're going to present, to make sure we don't have any holes or questions amongst ourselves. Think of it as our last prep session before our presentation. I'm sure you do something to prepare to play another team?"

"Got it, and yeah, we watch video from the last few games to see how they've been playing lately. What plays they like to run, or who's on a hot streak."

"Then think of this as our video session, but you know, just not watching videos unless it is a production video that is part of our presentation."

"Got it. Can you call them on your way in and at least talk amongst yourselves?" I suggest.

"Not a bad idea; maybe I will."

"Glad I could be of some help." I wink in her direction as we wait for the light to flip green. It finally does, and seconds later, I'm pulling into the parking lot of her condo building. "I'll walk you up," I state as I kill the engine.

"It really isn't necessary," she protests, but I ignore it and get out of the car anyway. She meets me behind the car as we walk across the lot and to the door. A quick swipe of her key and we're inside the lobby, waiting on the elevator to descend to the ground floor.

Tori unlocks her door, opening it quickly. I know she's in a hurry, but I also don't want her to be so stressed all day. As soon as the door clicks shut behind the two of us, I pull her into my arms and plant a kiss on her lips. She's ridged, at first, but gives in and melts into my embrace. Her hands slide up my chest and around the back of my neck, sliding into the hair at my nape.

I know time is precious, so I break the connection after only a minute or so of kissing her. "That's better. Now go shower and get ready. I'll see what I can find for you to have for breakfast, and then I'll get out of your hair. Are you free for dinner tonight? I promise to keep it an early night. I fly out tomorrow morning bright and early, so I need to call it an early night myself."

"Maybe. Can I let you know later today?" she asks.

"Of course. But just remember, we both need to eat, and I'd really like your pussy as my dessert."

Tori's head falls back in a deep laugh. "I don't know why what you say shocks me sometimes, but it does."

"Just tell it like it is, and I don't think you mind me eating your pussy," I state, my eyebrow raising in question.

"I can't complain; you are well versed in that activity. Most guys are like a lost puppy, unable to find the clit, even with a roadmap pointing directly to it."

"What can I say? I paid attention in sex education." I shrug my shoulders.

Tori barks out another laugh. "So, it's all about the

sex education class and not your personal experience that's perfected your skills?"

"Oh, my experience has definitely fine-tuned my skills, but I also might have studied the female anatomy, in depth, so I wouldn't fumble and fuck something up for my future partners."

"Interesting." She purses her lips, thinking over what I've just said.

"Enough about my sex education; you need to shower and get off to work."

"Shit." She pushes out of my arms, stumbling to the bathroom down the hall. "I'll be out in a little bit," she says before walking in and closing the door. I stand still, just staring at the door, until I hear the water turn on.

I make my way into the kitchen, opening her fridge to see what I've got to work with to make her something for breakfast. Hopefully, something she can take in the car somewhat easily. I find some eggs, pre-cooked bacon, and some chopped veggies in a container.

I pull them all out and get to work on some scrambled eggs with the veggies sauteed into them. I rummage through a few cupboards and find some tortillas, which will work perfectly for some breakfast burritos. By the time I hear the bathroom door open, I've got two large breakfast burritos filled and wrapped up. I find the tin foil and even wrap Tori's in it to keep it warm and help keep everything together if she chooses to eat in the car.

"What smells so good?" she asks, walking into the kitchen.

"Breakfast burritos," I say as I point to hers on the counter. I've already eaten half of mine as I wait for her.

"They smell divine. I had everything you needed for these?" she asks, taking a peek at the one in my hand.

"Yep, all from your fridge and cupboard."

"Impressive. I didn't realize I had all of that in there."

"You did, and they were easy to pull together."

"Thank you. I'll take it with me in the car. I need to go finish getting ready so I can get out of here," she says before checking the time on her watch.

I stay put in the kitchen while she gets ready. I busy myself by cleaning the pan and utensils I used to make breakfast, leaving her kitchen just as spotless as it was before I entered.

"You didn't have to clean," she says as she gathers her things.

"It was no problem. Are you all ready to head to work?"

"I think I am, I'm probably forgetting something, but it will all work out later."

"Then, let me walk you out," I state.

Tori doesn't argue, she just gathers her things and we head out the door. She pauses for a second to lock up tight. Before we know it, we're down at the doorway. The one on the left will take me out to the parking lot, and the one on the right takes you into the building's garage.

"You'll let me know, later, if dinner works?" I ask as I pull her into my arms before she can get away for the day.

"I'll let you know. I just need to get a handle on my day and see how things go at work. Our meetings with the talent can sometimes go extremely quickly, but other times they can take forever."

"Totally understand; just text or call when you're done, and we can make plans from there. As I said, I can't be out super late with an early morning flight tomorrow."

"Okay," she agrees.

"You're going to kick ass in your presentation."

"Thank you; I should get going."

"Of course, I need to get to the rink, myself." I check my watch and realize I need to report within the next hour. I cup her cheeks and pull her in for a quick kiss. Our night together was amazing, and I don't want this morning's snafu to make her regret our time together or give her any reason to push me away.

CHAPTER 7
TORI

I can't believe I fell asleep at Aiden's last night. The multiple orgasms lulled me right to sleep, and I didn't think about the repercussions it would make for today.

I pull from my garage and start the commute into the office. I hit the button on my car's console to call the office so I can have my meeting over the phone on my way in.

"Good morning, this is Rebecca," I'm greeted.

"Morning, Rebecca, it's Tori. I'm running late but wanted to use my commute into the office to go over everything with the team. Can you gather everyone up and call me back?"

"Of course, give me five minutes and we'll be ready."

"Perfect, thank you," I tell her before the line goes dead. I merge onto the highway and hope the traffic stays light, so I make it before the big meeting starts at ten.

I grab the breakfast burrito Aiden made for me and carefully unwrap part of it as I drive. I don't usually like to eat and drive, but desperate times call for desperate measures sometimes. The first bite hits my taste buds and I'm shocked again Aiden is such a good cook. I could easily get spoiled by his expertise in the kitchen.

I've consumed about half of my burrito by the time my phone is ringing through my speakers. I press the button on my steering wheel to accept the call, and the sound of my team's chatter fills the car.

"Hey, everyone, sorry about this morning."

"No problem, we've got everything under control," Will, one of the guys on my team says. He's the senior most member under me and always has such great ideas. The four of them all really work well together and are easy to manage on a day-to-day basis. I really lucked out when I was promoted and given the team I was.

"Cassandra, do you want to start at the top and we can go from there?"

"Sure thing," she happily agrees. "I've got all the presentation slides set up, showing the merchandise we've selected to have on hand. I verified all numbers yesterday afternoon with vendors and have included that information on the slides, as well, along with projected sales data based on past tours," she goes into detail.

"Perfect. Sounds like you've got it well covered and detailed. Good job," I praise. "Quinn, you're up next."

"I've got the video presentation ready for the fan

zone experience area. It will hopefully knock their socks off with the virtual reality set up we've done, mocking the experience we hope every fan gets to experience before or after the concert. I've also made a suggestion we include a merchandise stand within the fan zone. I think this will help with the buildup that happens right inside the stadiums as fans file in. If they've already had the chance to purchase merchandise before entering, it should help with that."

"I do like the idea, as the buildup is usually one of the biggest complaints, as is running out of merchandise. We'll need to make sure by splitting the merchandise into multiple areas, they'll have enough workers, and we can accommodate that with the inventory."

"I considered those things, as well, but this is why I think it will work. The fan experience is outside the venue. If the same staff who will be manning the inside booths run the outside one before the gates open, then we don't have to have double the people. They can close down the outside one prior to the gates opening and move inside. This would also allow them to move merchandise inside, if needed." Quinn states.

"We can discuss further. My concern would be an overlap of the fan experience still being open after the gates open and or there being a line at the merchandise booth swithin it that is still there when gates open. It would really piss people off if they stood in line, only to be cut off and told they now had to go inside and wait in another line that might be even longer. So, it's a great idea, we just need to work on the logistics of pulling it off. Adding a few people to sell merchandise shouldn't be an issue. We can probably get away with using local event staff rather than only the road crew staffing the booths. If we have a couple from the road crew as the leads, they can easily manage a handful of others each night."

"I'll note your concerns," Quinn says. "Would you like me to bring them up in the meeting to see if anyone else has any idea on how to make it work?" he asks.

"Absolutely. The more minds we have working on it, the better. I'm sure we can come up with a solution, it will just take us talking it out to do so."

"Sounds good, I've got it noted."

"Let's table the discussion, for now. I'm about to pull into the parking garage, so I'll see you all shortly. I'm feeling confident about this meeting today, and most of the feeling is because of all the hard work the four of you have done to get us ready," I tell them, and it's the truth. I wouldn't be as strong of an employee as I am, if they weren't on my team.

⁂

TODAY'S MEETING WENT GREAT, THE BAND LOVED THE ideas we had, so we're moving forward. The five of us will actually head out on the road and travel to the first five tour stops, to make sure everything we've set up works to plan and no changes need to be made. We don't always get to do that, so it's a fun time when we do. It's a few months away before it kicks off, but still, something to look forward to.

I finally have a chance to collapse in my office chair;

all my meetings for the day are finished and I feel like I can finally breathe a sigh of relief. Starting my day out late, which caused me to miss my morning at the gym, really could have made my day a whole lot worse, but in the end, it was a good day.

My phone buzzes on my desk, so I reach for it to see who's texting me. My guess is it's either Avery or Aiden.

AIDEN

Just checking in to see how your meeting went. Did you kick ass like I told you you would?

We totally kicked ass. My team is the best ever!

I knew you would! Celebration dinner and drinks then? {winky face}

I suppose, but I have to sleep at home tonight, so no keeping me out all night.

But tying you to your own bed is okay? {devil face}

Just think of all the orgasms I can provide if I tie you down and eat your pussy all night.

You still there? Are your panties wet yet?

Still here, and no, they aren't wet...yet.

How many times should I make you come on my tongue? Five times?

You're incorrigible. And how in the hell are you just willy-nilly texting me about orgasms? Shouldn't you be lifting weights or slamming teammates up against the walls?

I already spent three hours in the weight room today. Between the cardio last night and what I hope to get in tonight, I'm good. Don't worry, sweetheart, I'm not about to lose my eight pack. {winky face} And we try not to slam each other up against the boards too much, don't want to take out my own guys in practice.

I can understand that. The not hurting each other on purpose part. Did you say THREE HOURS? My god, I'd be dead on the floor if I spent three hours in the gym on a daily basis.

Yeah, but you're, what, a buck fifteen? My career requires me to be in the best physical shape I can be in. It requires a lot of time in the gym and on the ice.

Definitely not that low, but my weight doesn't really matter in this conversation. I missed bootcamp this morning, but I'm sore enough as it is from the workout your cock gave me last night. Not sure I could have even made it through if I didn't oversleep today.

I'd take orgasms over the gym any day.

I roll my eyes at his comment, but I can't hold back the smile he puts on my face, either.

> I'm sure you would. What would your coach think about that?

> Eh, he might not like it, but he's also a guy and understands sometimes the head downstairs overrules the one upstairs.

> I can't stop shaking my head at you. And laughing.

> Laughing is good; at least you aren't cursing my name. I'd be concerned about the cursing, unless the cursing comes while I'm fucking you. But I digress. I need to stop talking about fucking you or I'm going to end up with a hard-on in the locker room, and that is never a pleasant place to have one of those.

> I can't imagine it would be.

> So, dinner tonight? I could come over and bring take-out, or we can order in once I get there. Or would you rather me cook you something? I'm open to any and all suggestions.

> Do you like sushi? I'm kind of craving it.

> I haven't found a roll I didn't like. What did you have in mind?

> My favorite place is only a few blocks from my condo. You could come over, and we could go there, then back to my place for dessert?

As long as we can agree you're my dessert. {winky face} Tell me what time to be there and it's a date.

> Can you be at my place around five thirty? I can call and get a table for six o'clock; it will give us a few minutes before we have to head out to find parking and such.

Done; I'll see you then.

I set my phone back on my desk and look up to see Rebecca standing in my doorway. "Oh, hi. Were you standing there long?" I ask.

"A couple of minutes, but it looked like a good conversation. I didn't want to interrupt."

"You're fine. Just this guy I've started seeing," I tell her.

"Ooh, tell me more," she gushes, and takes a seat across from me.

"It's new, like, really new. My best friend, Avery, started dating one of his friends. The day she introduced me to her boyfriend, he was hanging out with some of his friends at a bar, so we tagged along, and it is where I met Aiden. He was pretty charming, but I thought he was a total player, at first. He's turned out to be a really nice guy, nothing like I pegged him to be when I first met him."

"Is he why you were late this morning?" she asks, an eyebrow raised in question.

"Partially. I didn't intend on sleeping over at his house last night; it just kind of happened. Because I wasn't planning on it, I didn't set an alarm. My oh-shit alarm is what woke me up this morning, and by that time, there was no way I'd make it on time. He was so sweet, though. Drove me home, stayed while I showered and got ready, and made me some breakfast to bring in the car. We're going out for dinner tonight. I told him I can't do the all-night thing again, but he can't, either, as he leaves in the morning for a business trip." I realize I'm holding back his identity and he fact he's a hockey player. It wouldn't take much research to determine who he is if I mentioned he plays professional hockey and his name is Aiden. As far as I know, he's the only Aiden on the team, and they are the only professional hockey team in this area.

"Sounds promising, and a sexy man is never a bad reason to be late every once in a while."

"It was a night to remember, for sure." I can't help but smile at the memory of last night. The way he so expertly worked my body multiple times over.

"I take it from that smile, the sex was good." Rebecca smirks.

"Good doesn't even touch it. You know how guys are described in romance novels?" I ask.

"With cocks so big they won't fit, oral skills that blow your mind, and stamina lasting all night long?" she asks.

"Exactly. And I shit you not; it is exactly how I'd

describe last night. Like the man not only knew where the clit was, but he knew what to do with it."

"Damn, does he have any brothers?"

"Just a sister, sorry." I shrug.

"Sounds like you found yourself a unicorn. Probably shouldn't let him go. Unless he just hasn't shown his douche side, that is."

"Thankfully, I don't get any douche vibes from him. It doesn't mean that can't come out later, but you know I won't put up with that shit. Life's too short to deal with douche men."

"Amen to that," Rebecca agrees. "All right, well, I need to get out of here. Have a good night with the new man. I hope to see you in the office on time tomorrow," she teases and winks before standing to head out for the day.

I gather my own things, ready to call it a day. My drive home is uneventful, which doesn't happen often. Traffic is usually a bitch, I do live in California, after all, but today I must have some good luck as I'm home about fifteen minutes early.

I kick my heels off as soon as I'm in my condo. I don't usually mind them, but I spent a good amount of time on my feet today, so they're sore. I pull out a glass and the open wine bottle from my fridge. If there's any day that deserves a glass of wine, it's tonight.

I take my full glass and head for my bedroom. I relax on my bed, scrolling online as I enjoy the fruity liquid. I get lost in catching up on today's news when my phone chimes, as someone is calling from downstairs.

"Hello," I greet.

"It's Aiden," he says through the phone.

"Come on up," I tell him, and start to panic. I completely lost track of time and haven't done anything to get ready for our dinner date, including calling to get a table like I said I'd do. Hopefully, they won't be slammed tonight and can still get us in. If not, we can always order it to go and come back here to eat.

I head for my door once I hear him knock. I pause before reaching for the lock, taking a deep breath to calm my sudden flutter of nerves.

I open the door and find him standing there, looking like the handsome man he is. Chiseled jaw and impeccably dressed, even if he is just in a pair of dark wash jeans and form-fitting T-shirt.

"Evening," he greets as he steps over the threshold of my condo.

"Evening," I parrot. "I kind of zoned out after getting home from work and haven't gotten ready for dinner. I also got sidetracked and never got us reservations, so hopefully, they can get us in, or we can order food and bring it back here," I tell him.

"Sidetracked, huh," he says as he backs me up against the wall and pins me with his body. "What sidetracked you?" he asks as his lips find the tender side of my neck.

"You and Rebecca," I manage to say, but my words come out all breathily.

"Who's Rebecca?" he asks as he kisses down my neck.

"One of the girls on my team. She was standing in

my doorway while I was texting you and asked me who I was talking to that put such a big smile on my face, so I told her a little about you."

"Is that so? I hope it was only good things." He smirks and moves to kiss me on the lips.

I melt into his embrace. Opening for him at the first swipe of his tongue along the seam of my lips. I tug him closer, or as close as I can get him. His chest is hard against my soft. I don't miss the fact his cock is hard in the jeans and pressing into me.

Aiden breaks the kiss, sucking in a deep breath before pulling back. "If I don't put some space between us, we might not make it to dinner. We both need sustenance if we're going to make it through later." He winks.

"Are you sure you aren't a sex addict?" I ask.

"Only with you," he assures me.

"Okay, let me change quickly and slip on some shoes, and I'll be ready to go."

"Take your time; I'm ready when you are."

I disappear into my room and pull out my jeans and a casual shirt to change into. I slip my dress off and slide into my new outfit. I quickly stop in the bathroom to check my hair and makeup. I reapply some lipstick and a spritz of perfume to freshen up a little. I pull my sandals from the hall closet, and now I'm ready to head out for dinner.

"Ready?" I call out. I find Aiden sitting on the couch, watching his phone's screen.

"Yes," he says, and I don't miss how his eyes scan my body.

"Something wrong with my outfit?" I ask, looking down at what I put on. I didn't notice any stains when I looked myself over in the mirror.

"Not one thing; you just look good enough to eat." He smirks and makes his way over to me. He pulls me into his arms and kisses me softly. "Let's go before I just haul you over my shoulder and into bed."

"Caveman." I chuckle and pat his chest.

"It's all because of you," he insists as we head out the door. I stop to lock up, and away we go.

"Where exactly am I going?" he asks as he backs out of the parking spot.

"Take a right onto the road, about a mile or so down; we'll take another right."

"Easy enough," he states as he pulls out onto the road.

Once we're near the restaurant, I point out an open parking spot just a few doors up from where we're going. Finding a spot so close is usually impossible, but luck is on our side as a car pulled out just before we went through the light.

"Welcome to The Sushi Spot; how many for tonight?" the hostess asks.

"Just the two of us, but I forgot to call for a reservation. Can you fit us in?" I ask, hopeful.

"We can; it will just be about a ten-minute wait. Will that work?" she asks.

"No problem, thank you."

"You're welcome, and a name for the party?"

"Tori," I tell her, and she marks it down.

"Have a seat, or feel free to wait at the bar; we'll call you shortly."

"Thanks," I tell her as I back into Aiden's chest. "Did you want to wait here or grab a drink in the bar?"

"I'm fine with either, what would you prefer?" he asks.

"Let's grab a drink," I suggest, and he escorts me over to the bar. We find two seats together near the far end of the long bar.

"Evening, what can I get for the two of you?" the young man behind the bar asks as he sets down two cocktail napkins.

"I'll have the Sunset Punch," I tell him.

"And for you, Sir?" he addresses Aiden.

"I'll take whatever blonde ale you have on tap."

"Coming right up. Did you want to open a tab or cash out now?" he asks as he fills Aiden's glass of beer from the tap in front of us.

"We can settle up now," Aiden says and holds out some cash.

The guy moves to make my drink, setting it down before he takes the cash and returns with Aiden's change. I don't miss when Aiden leaves him a nice tip on the counter.

"Tori, party of two," the hostess calls out, and we both stand up and head her way. She shows us to our table and hands over the menu before returning to her place up front.

"Good evening, I'm Patrick, and I'll be serving you tonight; I see you have some fresh drinks from the bar already; can I get you anything else to drink at the moment, or are we good?" he asks.

"I'm good," I tell him, looking to Aiden to answer.

"All good here, as well."

"Do you need a minute to look over the menu? Or can I put in an appetizer to get you started?" he asks.

"Do you want an app?" Aiden asks me.

"The tempura platter is what I usually get. Do you want to share it?" I ask.

"Sounds good to me," he says and turns to Patrick. "We'll take the tempura platter, for now."

"Coming right up; I'll be back in a few minutes for your full order."

We both take a minute to look over the menu; I don't even know why I'm looking at it, as I'm a creature of habit and always order the same thing.

Patrick returns a few minutes later with our appetizer platter and takes our dinner order. Aiden and I fall into a comfortable conversation as the time passes, and we enjoy the meal together.

CHAPTER 8
AIDEN

I walk into my condo, tossing my keys on the kitchen counter before heading to my bedroom.

As I promised Tori, I left her place by midnight. I was almost late, as we were still in her bed together at a quarter to midnight, basking in the aftermath of sex. I can't seem to satisfy my desire for her, which hasn't happened before. I, like most guys, enjoy a healthy sex life, but there's just something about our connection that I can't get enough of. The next week away is going to suck and will require me to get reacquainted with my left hand again.

I walk into my bedroom and pull out my suitcase. It already has a few of my travel essentials, like my toiletries bag, but I take it out and into the bathroom to refill a few things before tossing it back into the suitcase. I pull out three suits, one I'll wear tomorrow, and the other two will be for later in the road trip. I don't always take a new one for each game, as we don't necessarily have to have them on for very long each day, but when we have longer flights, I like to have options.

I add in some lounge clothes, as well as a couple of pairs of shoes, and I'm good to go. In the morning, I'll add my charging station, and I'll be out the door. I grab my backpack and pull out my iPad so it can charge overnight, as well as download a couple of new movies to have on hand to watch if I need something to space out with. The planes we fly on are always equipped with Wi-Fi, but it isn't always reliable enough to watch a movie that isn't downloaded, so I've learned to be prepared. I head into the kitchen and grab a few of my protein bars and drink mixes to add to my bag. The team provides us with most of our stuff, but I like to have my own on hand, as well.

With everything ready for the morning, I strip out of my clothes and slide into bed. As soon as I'm flat on my back, my mind drifts to last night, and Tori is lying on the pillow next to me. Her body splayed out underneath me as I drove into her. The way she'd gasp with every thrust of my cock as it hit her deep inside. The memories have my cock swelling and lengthening, wishing I was still next to her so I could pull her on top of me and slide her wet center down my cock.

I wrap my fist around my length, giving it a few long and slow strokes as I think about her sweet pussy. The way she rode my face tonight as she came over and over. I speed up my strokes, twisting around my crown as I kick the covers off, so I don't blow my load all over them. I imagine sucking her perfectly hard nipples into my mouth as I finger fuck her. The idea of making her come so hard she squirts all over my hand has my orgasm barreling to the edge, ready to crest over as I pump harder and faster. I can just imagine it now; I'd eat her pussy until she's come twice—no, three times. Get her nice and wet and so sensitive she will come a fourth time with little effort. I'll slide a few fingers inside and twist them in a come-hither motion, all while blowing lightly on her clit. The sensation of my breath should set her off and maybe—just maybe, have her squirting in pleasure. The moment, the idea of her cresting over the edge of ecstasy, has my own orgasm barreling out of me. My cock stiffens as my cum coats my abs. I'm a little shocked I came this hard again after the evening we already had together, but I'm damn near unstoppable with Tori in my life. I reach for a tissue on the nightstand and wipe my abs off before I head into the bathroom for a quick rinse-off shower and back to bed for my early morning wakeup.

I BOARD THE TEAM PLANE AND TAKE MY SEAT. WE DON'T have assigned ones, but hockey players tend to be creatures of habit. We're also superstitious as fuck, so I end up next to Ryker. Tristan and Damien, one of our defense pairs, are in the seats across from us. They both give me chin lifts as I take my seat.

"Hey, man, how's your morning?" Ryker asks as I get settled into my seat.

"Can't complain. Didn't want to get out of bed when

the alarm went off, but I'm here," I tell him as I bring the disposable coffee cup to my lips.

"Out late?" he asks.

"Got home just after midnight," I tell him.

"Who is she?" he asks. I've kept my mouth shut in the locker room. Some guys like to boast about the women they're dating or fucking. It's usually the ones that are bed hopping who are the most vocal.

I turn to look at him before I answer. "Tori," I say, and wait for the name to ring a bell.

"No shit, you actually got her to agree to a date?"

"A couple of dates, now." I smirk. "And maybe more," I tell him, and hope I'm not jumping the gun.

"Maybe?" he questions, his eyebrows pulling together in question.

"She wants to take things slow, and I'm fine with it. I did lay it all on the line that I'm not a player. I don't bed hop, and I don't like to share. So, if we're sleeping together, then we're only sleeping with each other."

"Nothing wrong with those kinds of terms."

"It's still new; hell, we've only just gone out twice this week. There's something there, man. I just know it."

"Then be patient. Don't rush it if it feels like she's the one."

"I'm trying. I can't get enough of her. She's just so easy to be around. We get along great, both in and out of the bedroom. She doesn't seem to be fazed by my career or the travel required of us."

"All good stuff, but I wouldn't expect much different from Avery's best friend. I haven't known her long, myself, since she was out of the country when Avery and I first met, but she seems pretty cool, and I know Aves couldn't imagine not having her in her life. Happy for you, man; just don't fuck it up. I don't need my girl mad at me because you hurt her best friend."

I laugh at his quasi-threat, knowing he wouldn't ever do anything to hurt me. "Don't plan on it. If anything, she'll be the one to break my heart," I tell him.

"Damn, you are already head over heels, aren't you?" he asks.

"Possibly," I state. "I can't articulate it. It's like she's my magnet. I'm only pulled in her direction and constantly feel a pull to go to her when apart."

"Damn, dude, you've got it bad if you're already feeling like this, and it hasn't even been a week. Are you sure it isn't the excessive amount of sex? Because by the look of you, she's wrung you out and left you to dry." He laughs at my expense.

"Fucker," I mumble under my breath. "Like you and Avery didn't have a sex-filled weekend not long after you guys stopped the avoidance dance."

"Fuck, yes, we did. One of the best weekends of my life." He smirks.

"That's how the last two nights have been, except we both had to function at work during the day."

He grimaces. "Y'all need a weekend away, but good luck finding one anytime soon. I don't think we have a game-free weekend until the all-star break."

I groan. "Fucking sucks, but it is what it is. Maybe

we can take a mid-week getaway before then when we have a couple of days off."

"Might work," he states before we're interrupted by the flight attendant, who is offering everyone coffee or orange juice before we take off. One nice thing about flying on chartered jets is the food and drink are a lot better than on commercial airlines. Since this is an early morning flight, once we're in the air, they'll serve us breakfast and, later on, lunch.

We land in Buffalo by late afternoon. The time change, plus the five-hour cross-country flight, takes its toll on us. It's why we flew out a day early. Helps us get acclimated to the time change and work out some of the stiffness from our legs.

The charter bus takes us directly to the hotel, where the team has already checked us in. Davis, one of the office staff members, boards the bus and hands out the keycards to everyone, room numbers labeled on the little packets the keys are in.

"Dinner will be ready in about forty-five minutes in conference room A on the second floor," Davis informs us before we all gather our carry-on bags and exit the bus. Our suitcases have already been unloaded and are waiting for us to grab and take with us as we enter through the back entrance of the hotel.

Once in my room, I have a set routine I like to go through. Unpack the suitcase, hanging my suits up, first, so they don't wrinkle. Change out of the suit I was required to travel in and put on either sweats or joggers and a T-shirt, or some athletic shorts and a T-shirt. Just depends on the weather and what we've got going the rest of the travel day. Since we won't leave the hotel tonight, joggers it is.

I drop my bathroom bag on the counter before doing my business and heading to rest for a few minutes on the bed. Hotels can definitely be hit or miss on their comfort level. They don't put us up in dives, by any means, but just because it is an expensive hotel doesn't mean the bed or pillows will be comfortable.

I flip the TV on, mainly for the background noise, as I scroll through my phone. I've got a missed text from my sister; just checking in to see how my week's going and wishing me luck in tomorrow's game.

I hit her contact and the speakerphone button as it rings.

"How's my favorite brother tonight?"

"Last I checked, I'm your only brother." I smile as this is a very normal exchange between the two of us.

"Hence, why you're my favorite."

"I'm good, just got into the hotel a few minutes ago. Just stretched out on the bed and called you," I tell her.

"Let me guess, you've hung up your suits, changed clothes, and are now relaxing until dinnertime?"

"I'm that predictable, huh?" I chuckle.

"Um, yeah. I think you've had the routine, now, for at least five years, maybe longer."

"What's the saying, don't fix what isn't broken."

"Hockey players and their superstitions," she says, and I can just imagine the eye roll that accompanied it. "How'd your date with Tori go?" she asks, changing the subject.

"Good, great, actually. We had a second one last night since the first one went so well."

"How exciting!" she squeals. I'm glad I had the phone on speaker, as I'm sure my eardrums would have been blown out had I been holding the phone to my ear.

"I really like her, Sis. There's something special about this one," I tell her honestly.

"That makes me so happy. I'm happy for you and wish the two of you the best. She seemed really nice after the game the other night, and I like how she called you out, thinking you were playing me."

"She's one of the good ones. My career and subsequent income don't matter to her. I've never asked directly, but I don't think she's living paycheck to paycheck, either, based on her job title, employer, and the nice condo she's got."

"Not being a gold digger is a huge plus. I've worried a lot that whom you'd end up with would only be after the zeros in your bank account and not in the relationship for you. It's nice to hear you might have actually found a woman who is like that."

"Only time will tell; she still wants to take things slow. We'll see how things are after I've been gone a week and am not around daily."

"Nothing wrong with a little space, especially if she wants to take things slow. Maybe the separation will help her see just how much she likes you and enjoys your company. Plus, everyone needs a little space once in a while. Your job forces space every other week, basically, so learn to live with it."

"I'm very accustomed to the travel schedule, it's

Tori; I'm not sure I can handle it. But as you said, only time will tell."

"Keep me posted, and I hope everything works out the way you want it to."

"Thanks, Sis. How are things for you?" I ask, turning the conversation away from my love life.

"Same shit, different day."

"Better than shit hitting the fan daily." I chuckle.

"I can't argue with that," she says.

"Hey, someone's knocking at the door, so I'm sure it's one or more of the guys wanting to head down for some food; I'll call you in a few days."

"Sounds good, and have a good game tomorrow. Love you," she says.

"Love you, too, Amy," I tell her before hitting the end button and opening the door.

"Who are you professing your love to?" Tristan asks.

"My sister, asshole." I smack the back of his head as he enters my room.

"Oh, sorry. I thought you were confessing your love to some chick."

"Does it scare you, little boy?" I tease him.

"Gives me fucking hives just thinking about it. I'm going to be single until I die."

"Careful putting that out into the universe; some girl might come in and flip you upside down, and you'll be begging her to settle down with you," Ryker tells him.

"And give up all the free pussy, no thanks," he says, waving off Ryker's advice.

"I'm going to remember this conversation and love

it when I get to say I told you so; mark my words, boys."

"Enough about that shit, let's go eat. I'm starving," Tristan says.

We file out of my room and run into Damien and one of our goalies, Blake. "I'm taking the stairs; I need the movement in my legs," I call out as we walk down the hall.

"Not a bad idea," Ryker says as we reach the elevator area, as well as the door for the stairwell. The other guys follow us, deciding they can run the stairs with us down the four floors to where we need to go for dinner.

We easily find the conference room the hotel has set aside for us to use for meals. The long buffet is set up, a few guys already at it, filling their plates high with a few pasta options, along with what looks like grilled chicken and roast beef. I grab two plates from the stack, filling the first one with a large salad, the second with a healthy helping of pasta and a couple of chicken thighs.

"Anyone know the schedule for tomorrow?" I ask, once most of us sit at one of the large round tables.

"Breakfast is in here at seven, bus leaves for the morning skate at eight thirty, we'll return at eleven thirty, and lunch should be ready when we get back. We leave for the rink at four fifteen," Ryker tells everyone.

"Ten-four, Cap," Blake calls out, and the room erupts in laughter. Being a new team, we're all still getting to know one another on a deeper level. Friend-ships are forming. Not that we're cliquish, but guys tend to gravitate toward each other, and deeper friend-ships are formed.

I dig into my food, my body is so messed with the time zone I'm in, I'm surprised I'm as hungry as I am. Once we're all done, most of us hang around the room, bull shitting with one another until guys are ready to call it a night and get some sleep or head back to the rooms to check in with family back home.

"I'm out," Ryker says, checking the time on his watch. "Ellie should be home, and I want to check in with her, see how her test went today," he tells me.

I hop up from my seat and stretch my tired body. "I'll walk back up with you," I tell him.

"Night," I call to the small group of guys still hanging out.

"Have you talked to Tori since we got in?" Ryker asks as we take the stairs back up.

"No, I called my sister as soon as I unpacked, earlier, and talked to her until you showed up. But she also hasn't tried to contact me, either, so maybe she doesn't want to hear from me?" I question.

"Are you afraid to find out?" he asks, and I ponder his question for a few steps.

"Nah, I'll call her once I'm back in my room. I think she had another busy day at work, so she might not have had the time to try and reach out; plus, I told her it would be late when we got in, settled, and had dinner."

"All right, take it a day at a time, and I'm sure things will work out the way they're supposed to, man."

"Thanks," I tell him as we arrive at my door. Ryker waves and continues down the hall to his own room.

Our entire team fills up every room on this floor between all the players, coaches, and the training and equipment people. Depending on the hotel, we sometimes need multiple floors, but the front office prefers when they can book at a hotel large enough to dedicate an entire floor to us. It makes securing it a little easier. People, mainly single women, will try and sneak their way into guys' rooms. They've been successful in the past. Not with this team, but with prior ones I've played on, and gotten a guy or two into some dicey situations.

I kick my runners off once I'm in my room and flop down on the bed. I hit the mute button to silence the TV and then click on Tori's contact. I consider for a moment that I should have texted her, first, but too late now.

The phone rings three times before it connects. "Hello," she greets, and I'm transported right to her front door in my mind.

"Evening, beautiful. How was your day?" I ask.

"Busy, how was yours?"

"Eh, just tiring. Flight was good, no hiccups with getting to the hotel. Just got back to my room from dinner and BSing with the guys."

"Are you in for the night, then?" she asks.

"Yep," I say and cover a yawn. "It's already ten here. We've got breakfast at seven and will head to the rink for morning skate just after eight," I tell her.

"Oh, wow. I didn't realize you'd have to go to the rink so early on a game day."

"When we're at home, morning skates are optional. Some guys love them, as it helps loosen up their legs if they get out on the ice for a short amount of time, usually thirty or so minutes. Some never touch the ice before pre-game warm-ups. It also gives us a time we can see the trainers for any ailments we want some help with. On road trips, morning skates can be important, as we're on airplanes for long stretches of time, and it makes the legs cramp up. I'm hit or miss on attending morning skate at home, but I usually will get out for a little bit when we travel to make sure I don't need anything worked on," I explain.

"And then what happens? Because the game isn't until tomorrow, right?" she asks.

"Yeah." I chuckle, almost loving how little she knows about hockey.

"After our morning skate, we head back to the hotel, have some lunch, and then it's nap time."

"Nap time? Like a toddler?" she asks, and I can hear the humor in her voice.

"Exactly. Don't let my size fool you; I'm just a big-ass baby in a man's body and clothes."

"I knew you were hiding something from me," she laughs, and I wish I were next to her.

"We take a nap, or most guys do. Then, it's up by late afternoon and off to the rink. We get there a few hours before game time. We need to stretch, eat, warm up, have a team meeting if our coach calls one, stretch some more, hit the ice for warm-ups, and finally, game time."

"I'm exhausted just listening to everything. And you do this day after day," she states more than questions.

"Sometimes, but we also get days off between games, usually."

"You're in Buffalo tonight, but you play New Jersey on Sunday, so when do you head down there?" she asks.

"Our flight will take off about two hours after the game ends tomorrow night."

"Oh, wow, so they keep you guys moving. Why not just wait until the morning to fly?"

"They'd rather us get into the new hotel and settled. Even if it means flying overnight. We won't have any required practice on Saturday but will probably have some optional ice time in the afternoon. When we have a full off day like this weekend, a lot of times, we'll go out to dinner as a team somewhere nice."

"Fun, and will you leave there as soon as your game ends on Sunday?" she asks.

"Nope. New Jersey and two of the New York teams all play within a few miles of each other, so when we come to town and play all of them, we stay put at the same hotel. So, once we make it to New Jersey, we'll be in that hotel until Wednesday night when we fly back home. We have back-to-back games on Tuesday and Wednesday nights. But since there isn't any travel between cities, it really isn't that big of a deal to be playing two different teams back-to-back."

"That's cool. Knock out three teams without leaving the area. I'm surprised there are so many teams so close to each other."

"It's New York City and Jersey; there are a shit ton of people in the area."

"I guess you're right. How many teams are in California?" she asks.

"Four with the addition of the Shockwaves," I tell her.

"Are they all spread out?"

"Kind of. There is a team in LA and one in Anaheim. They are kind of close by one another. When we play them back-to-back, we move hotels, but it's more of a traffic issue with getting to the rinks on time. We also won't always play them in the same trip since they are within the same state."

"So interesting. I can't even imagine being in charge of the travel logistics of a sports team."

"Says the woman who helps plan world tours for bands."

"Most of the crews all sleep on the busses, so we aren't booking hotels up in very many cities. Sometimes the bands will want to stay in a hotel if they have a few days in a city, but they typically make those decisions as they go and have personal assistants or tour managers who make all those types of calls on the fly."

"Still, you make it sound like what you do isn't cool shit."

"I guess." She sighs. "Oh, did I tell you, I get to travel for a few shows with one of the bands. The one we had that big meeting with the other day."

"You didn't, but it sounds like you're excited about the opportunity?"

"Yes! I travel sometimes, but it's usually just to a tour stop somewhere here in California. But since we're testing out some new ideas with this tour, we want to observe and help out with them for the first handful of shows to make sure our ideas work out the way we've planned and can implement them on other tours."

"Awesome; when will that be?" I ask.

"The tour starts late January, so we'll probably fly out a day or two early to meet up with everyone, then it will be the partial road life for a couple of weeks."

"Why partial?" I ask.

"Still not clear if my team will fly between cities or if we'll rent an extra tour bus for us."

"Do you have a preference?"

"Both options have pros and cons. The tour bus would probably be a tad bit easier, as we wouldn't have to deal with commercial flights or the corporate jet availability."

"Can they not charter a small commuter jet for the few weeks?" I ask.

"I'm sure they could, but as I said, a bus might be easier. We're working on figuring out the logistics, and if a bus is available for the two-ish weeks, we'd need it during that time. Some drivers won't take short assignments like what we need. It's why we're already working on it and getting all our ducks in a row."

"Gotcha; well, I hope it all works out for you."

"Thanks, we're pretty stoked. No one else on my team has ever traveled on a tour, so this will be a new experience for all of them."

"Very cool," I state. "Not to change the subject, but do you have plans a week from today?" I ask.

"I can't think of anything; why, did you have something in mind?" she asks, and I swear her voice switches to a seductive tone.

"You, me, dinner, and your pussy on my face would be a good start. Not necessarily in that order."

"Why, Mr. Fox, you have a way of propositioning me." She giggles. "How can I turn down an offer like that?"

"My goal was to offer something so good you couldn't say no to it," I tell her, a smile tugging at the edges of my lips.

"It's a date. What time should I expect you?"

"How early can you be home? We'll get back around two a.m., so I won't try and bother you then, unless you want me to."

"Let me check my schedule and see if I can play hooky that day, or at least leave early."

"I like the sound of that; if you play hooky, I might just show up on your doorstep when we fly back in. Start our day off early." My cock twitches, just thinking about the possibility.

"It's too bad there's no way for me to get into your condo, so I could be waiting in bed for you," Tori states.

"I can make it happen. You just tell me it's an option, and you can definitely be waiting in my bed for me, but only if you're naked when I get there."

"Last time, you wanted to take my panties off with your teeth, now, you want me naked. Can you make up your mind on what you prefer," she teases.

"Different times call for different options."

"Okay, I'll try and figure out tomorrow if I can take the day off next week and let you know for sure."

"Even if you can't, you're more than welcome to be waiting in my bed for me. I'll make it well worth your while and lack of sleep."

"I'm sure you will." She snickers.

"What are you wearing right now?" I ask suddenly.

"The slacks and blouse I wore to work, why?" she asks, obviously confused with the sudden subject change.

"Talking and thinking of you naked and in my bed has me thinking about what I want to do to you, and has my cock so fucking hard, I'm going to have to rub one out before I can fall asleep tonight. Figured a little visual stimulation wouldn't hurt the cause."

"Are you touching yourself right now?" she asks.

"Definitely. I've got my fist wrapped around my cock. It's heavy and hard, all for you."

"God damn, you are going to drive me crazy. I can't do this. Not right now. Not yet," she states, and I can tell she's a little uncomfortable with the phone sex direction this conversation is headed.

"Then we won't," I tell her matter-of-factly. "I'm not here to push you into anything you're uncomfortable with, Tori. Much like after our first date for drinks, I'm willing to take what you're willing to share with me. No hard feelings. I can deal with a hard cock. I've done it before, and I'll do it again."

"Really?" she questions, and I can hear the shock in her voice. "Just like that?"

"Just like that. If you say no, it means no. I won't try and change your mind or push. It means you've set a boundary, and I won't cross it unless or until you tell me any different. I know it might be shocking, but I'm not most guys, Tori. I respect women, especially one I'm pursuing in the manner I'm pursuing you."

"You're one of a kind, do you know that, Aiden Fox?" she asks. "I'm truly blown away by the upstanding man you are. You are constantly showing me different sides of you, and I haven't found one yet I don't admire and find sexy."

"I'm glad I've made such an impression. I hope I keep up the standard I've set so far and don't disappoint you."

"I'm not sure there's much you could do to disappoint me, at this point. Unless you're running an underground dog fighting club or baby smuggling ring or some random shit like that, I'm extremely impressed with what I've seen so far."

"Good, let's keep it that way," I tell her. "On a lighter note, I should probably attempt to get some sleep. My alarm is going to come early, and I need a good night's sleep. I was up a bit late last night; someone's pussy was needing my attention."

"Lucky pussy." She laughs. "Good night, have a good day tomorrow. Text or call if you have time and want to chat. I don't have any meetings, so I'll be available almost all day, unless something pops up."

"I'll do that, have a good night, and talk soon," I say before ending the call.

I head for the shower; might as well relieve the pressure of my cock where it's easiest to clean up. Maybe after a nice hot shower and an orgasm, I'll be able to fall asleep quickly and get a good night's sleep.

CHAPTER 9
TORI

"It's girls' night!" Avery calls out as she stands in her open doorway, watching me as I walk off the elevator and down the hall to her condo. She lives right next door to Ryker, hence how they met and are now an item.

"Bring it on, bestie!" I holler as I hold up the bottle of wine I have in one hand and the takeout bag in the other. "Is Ellie joining us?" I ask as I walk into her place.

"She ditched us for her best friend. They're having a sleepover at her friend's house tonight. Last weekend was here; this weekend is there. I have a feeling they will just keep switching back and forth all year."

"Sounds like a good plan, so with no young ears around, it's time for you to dish." I give her a pointed look.

"Me? I need all the juicy details about you and Aiden." She gives me a pointed look right back. "I've got the channel on; the game feed should start any minute now. They don't always show the warm-ups, but they usually at least have it in the background while the TV people talk endlessly about stats and other games going on around the league."

"Before we start gabbing or sit down to watch the game, I need some food, so let's eat," I suggest. I had a rushed lunch today and didn't get to eat much during my break.

I set out the containers from a local Chinese place around the block. I ordered a big family meal deal they have, as it includes all Avery and my favorites. We do this occasionally, and it gives us food to gorge on all night long as we sit up and gab, do our nails and some skin treatments, or just sit around and drink wine and eat our weight in Chinese food.

"God, this is so good." Avery moans as she bites into a crab Rangoon.

"I know. So good!" I exclaim as I take a bite of the cashew chicken. It is probably my ultimate favorite dish they have, and that is saying something because I love just about everything they serve.

We take our full plates and wine glasses with us to the living room, getting comfortable on the couch. Just as we sit down, the channel starts the feed of the Shockwaves game. The national anthem is being sung by some up-and-coming newbie singer I've heard of in the last few months. She's pretty good; young, but good. I can only hope the industry doesn't ruin her like it has so many other young women.

Once the anthem is done, the lights come back on, and the camera pans out to show the guys skating around a bit, as well as panning the length of both benches, showing all the players as they take their spots and wait for the puck to drop.

I watch in amazement as the two guys line up at center ice, each placing their sticks ever so perfectly on either side of the circle painted in the middle. They don't take their eyes off the puck being held up by the referee. As soon as the whistle blows, he drops the puck, and they both go after it. I can't take my eyes off the screen as we watch the Shockwaves gain possession of the puck and skate it down the ice. Watching the game on TV is so different than watching it in person. I kind of like it this way, as I have the commentators telling me what exactly is happening. Ellie has done a great job explaining things to Avery and me when we've gone, but this is a little different. Hearing the plays called is a new experience, and one I'm actually enjoying.

"Okay, now that the first period is over, spill it, woman. I want to know everything!" Avery exclaims as she prods my shoulder.

We shift on the couch, so we're facing one another. She turns the TV down, so the intermission show isn't a distraction.

"I don't even know where to start, Aves. It's been a whirlwind since the game the other night."

"So, start there. What happened after the game? You left with him, correct?"

I recap everything. From the moment we left the rink to our short text conversation we had this afternoon when he checked in for a few minutes after waking up from his afternoon nap.

"Did you know hockey players took afternoon naps on game day?" I ask her, still tickled about that piece of knowledge.

"I did; it's pretty funny to think about, right?"

"I actually asked him if he meant like a toddler," I say, hardly getting it out between my belly laughs.

"You didn't!" Avery exclaims and smacks her knee as she laughs hard.

"I totally did. He was such a smart ass with his reply, but it was all in good fun."

"I'm so happy for you; I hope it all works out. He seems like such a great guy."

"I'm still apprehensive, but optimistic at the same time. Does that make any sense, or am I the biggest oxymoron there is?" I ask.

"I don't think being apprehensive but optimistic is a bad thing. I actually think it's good. There's nothing wrong with protecting yourself when it comes to a new relationship. I was worried about progressing things further with Ryker, especially since I was helping him with Ellie, but we took the leap, and look at us now. Living our best lives with each other."

"Yeah, he asked me if I could take Thursday off from work. Be at his place when they fly back home in the wee hours of the morning and then spend all day together. Knowing him, he'll want to spend it all in bed, but I can't say I'd complain much." I can feel my cheeks burn red, but this is my best friend. We've discussed our sex lives for years, so nothing's changing now.

"Can you make it work?" she asks.

"I actually can. I've got some PTO I need to burn up,

and the end of next week is pretty clear, schedule-wise. I could take off Thursday and Friday and have a nice long weekend to relax and get shit done."

"Sounds like you've just answered your own question." She smirks at me.

"What are you doing on Friday? I'm guessing the guys would have to go to practice or something. Aiden only talked about being off on Thursday."

"They have a home game Friday night, so it would be optional skate, afternoon naps, and reporting to the rink around four thirty or so."

"Do you want to have a spa day? I can get us appointments for a day package, and we can make a day of it."

"Um, yes. I won't say no to a day at the spa. Maybe we can end our day by going to the game? Just eat at the rink or grab something on our way?"

"Yeah, we can just wing it; I'll see what time I can get appointments, and then we can plan better."

Avery takes a large drink of her wine. "Perfect; I can't wait. I need a self-care day and spending it with you sounds even better."

"I couldn't agree more. We need to make a better effort with self-care days. We don't have nearly enough of them."

"Isn't that the truth?"

The game comes back on, and our attention is drawn back to the TV. The game has kind of been a boring one. Not many penalties have been called, and they are tied at two goals each, so the whistle has blown very little so far in the game. One of the teams needs to step it up and get some more goals. I can only hope it is the Shockwaves who find all the luck during the second period.

The game ends in a shootout, the Shockwaves coming out as the winner, which I know will make Aiden happy. I'm sure he won't like it took going to a shootout to win, but it's still a win at the end of the day.

I cover a large yawn. All my late nights and early mornings are catching up with me. I find myself zoning out occasionally when I should be working, and it's going to cause a problem if I'm not careful.

"Are you headed home, or did you want to crash here?" Avery asks as we both start to clean up from dinner. We did as I expected and binged right away on the food and then grazed at it the rest of the night.

"I think I'll head home. Nothing against your guest bed, but I need mine tonight."

"No hard feelings," she chuckles, "I totally get it. I'd want to come home to sleep in my bed if the roles were reversed."

"Thanks for understanding."

"Of course, what are friends for?"

"Did you want to grab some brunch tomorrow?" I ask.

"Maybe, I'll need to check with Ellie before I commit to anything," she says.

"Bring her along! The more, the merrier."

"Text me when you get up, and I'll let you know; how does that sound?" Avery asks.

I pull my best friend into a hug. "Works for me, and thanks for tonight. It was just what I needed."

"You know you're welcome here anytime. It was long overdue, so I'm glad it worked out. I also like having someone else to watch games with. Just think of all the WAG things we can do together if the two of you get serious."

"WAG?" I question.

"It stands for wives and girlfriends. The guys are together so much their significant others tend to form a tight-knit group and plan things. Sometimes for home games and get-togethers while the guys are on the road. No one understands what it's like to be with a hockey player better than other significant others."

"Ah, yeah, I guess I didn't even think of that aspect of dating a player. Have you met all the others?"

"Most of them. Not all the guys are in relationships, but the ones who are and that I've met have all been really nice."

"That's great; sounds like it would be a fun group to be a part of."

"At the next home game, I'll introduce you to the group."

"Is going to every home game a requirement?" I wonder, as it could possibly be a problem.

"Of course not. The players can get their family a season pass, but you aren't required to use it. They understand we have lives outside of their schedule. Some of the girls only come to weekend games or every-other if they play at home for a string of them. Especially the guys with younger kids, it is a lot on the moms and is usually way past their bedtimes."

"I didn't even think of that aspect. Does Ellie go to all the games?"

"No, because of how early she needs to be up for school; she's only gone to the weekend ones, so far, plus watched some of the road games with me since they're usually on early here with the time differences."

"She seems to be pretty responsible and studious."

"She's great; I've really enjoyed getting to know her. Dating a man with a fifteen-year-old daughter is a little nerve-racking. I remember what it was like to be fifteen. I'm just glad she isn't a bratty teenager who goes out of their way to make my life miserable, because if she was, I don't think I would have pursued the relationship with Ryker."

"I don't blame you; a bratty teenager sounds miserable. I'm so happy for you that it's working out. You deserve it all, and from the little I've seen you with Ryker, he sure does make you smile."

"Yeah, he's pretty great." She sighs, and I can practically see the heart eyes forming.

"All right, I think we've gotten everything cleaned up, so I'm going to get out of here so I can get home and to bed. I'll talk to you tomorrow."

"Drive safe, and I'll text Ellie to find out what her plans are for tomorrow, plus see if she wants to do brunch with us."

"Perfect, love you, goodnight," I tell her as I give her another hug before heading out the door.

Once home, I drop my things on the kitchen counter and head for my bathroom. All the liquid I consumed at Avery's is ready to burst out of me by the time I make it.

Once done, I decided to fill up my soaking tub and relax for a little while before climbing into bed. I crank up the hot water and drop in a bath bomb to start fizzing as the tub fills up. I head into my bedroom and grab my kindle, phone, and robe before returning to the bathroom.

While the tub continues to fill up, I grab the tray that sits across my tub and will hold my kindle, phone, a drink if I want it, as well as a snack if I'm so inclined. I get everything settled into place, then strip out of my clothes.

I step into the tub, the hot water instantly relaxing my body as I sink down into it. The bubbles from the bath bomb all surround me as I get comfortable. I adjust the pillow behind me, then turn on my kindle and pull up the new release, which just hit my account earlier this week.

I've only read the first chapter when my phone buzzes in the holder. A picture I snapped of Aiden and me the other night fills the screen, so I answer the phone.

"Hey," I say, the sound a little echoey in the bathroom.

"Where are you?" he asks.

"At home in my tub," I tell him. The water sloshes as I move slightly, making it even more obvious where I am.

Aiden groans. "New fantasies unlocked."

I giggle at his statement. I wasn't going for that kind of teasing, but I can easily see how he'd take it that way.

"Sorry, but a relaxing bath sounded like the perfect

way to end the long week. I had a fun night with Avery. We gorged on Chinese food, watched your game, and caught up with each other."

"Sounds like a good time, but tell me more about this watching my game part," he states, and I can tell he's happy I watched.

"I actually enjoyed it. Having the commentators explaining what was going on was a whole new experience for me. Ellie did a great job explaining things to me at my first game, but this was just different."

"I'm glad you enjoyed it."

"Are you guys flying out soon?" I ask.

"Yeah, I'm just waiting on the bus, now. A few more guys are still inside, getting ready. We should be headed to the airport in the next fifteen minutes or so," he says, and I can hear him yawning.

"Tired?" I ask.

"Yeah, I didn't get much rest during my afternoon nap; plus, with the game going all the way into a shootout, it makes our night much later. We probably won't get to our hotel until two, if we're lucky. Thankfully, we have tomorrow off, so I can sleep in and rest for most of it. I think Ryker made reservations at some steakhouse for all of us tomorrow night."

"I hope you get some rest," I tell him as I move the water around a little.

"I can't get the idea of you naked in the tub out of my mind," he admits. "I wish I was there with you."

"Maybe next weekend," I suggest. "I love a good long soak in the tub after a long day or week. I've got my kindle fired up, a new smutty book loaded, and I'm ready to relax."

"A smutty book, huh?"

"Yep," I state, popping the p. "One of my favorite authors released a new book this week, and I haven't had the chance to start it until tonight."

"Like, how smutty are we talking, here?"

"The full Monty, multi-page sex scenes, full descriptions, not a fan of fade-to-black-type of romances. I know that's what some people prefer, but not me. I want the details. Give me all of the sexy details," I tell him.

"Any chance you'd want to reenact one of these sex scenes out one day?" he asks.

"Maybe." I shrug, even though he can't see me.

"You should text me a link to the book, and I'll download a copy to brush up on some suggestions, unless you have one in mind already for us to try."

"Hmm, I could send you the link, but I also have some ideas forming," I tell him.

"Oh, yeah? What might they be?" he asks.

"This didn't come from a book, but from a TikTok video I saw. This man walked up to his girlfriend or wife and told her to fold her hands like she was praying, but to leave the fingers of one of her hands up and not curled around the others. He slipped his own hand into hers, linking their fingers. He then raised them up above her head, and because her hands were locked together, he now had control of both of hers. He backed her up against the wall and kissed her. I'm sure I'm not doing it any justice in explaining how it worked, but I just remember thinking, I wish I had a man who would back me up against the wall and ravish me."

"Sounds simple enough," he states. "What other kind of fantasies do you have?"

"Lots of them, but I'm not sure I'm ready to share anymore tonight," I tell him.

"That's okay; you can share when you're ready. But send me the link, I have lots of downtime, and I can for sure read a smutty book if it will give me any insight into the way your brain processes things."

"Are you sure? It's pretty smutty," she asks.

"I'm one thousand percent committed to reading a romance book. Just tell me what one or which ones I should read, and I'll get them downloaded."

"I just texted you a link to the first book in the series I'm on. If you enjoy that one, just continue on; the link for the next one will be at the end."

"I'll download it before we take off," he tells me.

"Your teammates won't give you shit about reading it?" I ask.

"It's not like I'll be holding a paperback with a half-naked guy on the cover. I'll have it on my iPad. If it makes you feel any better, I can wait to read it when I'm in my room."

"I'd just hate to give the guys something to tease you about, and I can't see a locker room full of guys not giving another guy shit about reading a romance novel."

"Eh, they'd probably crack a joke or two, or razz me for a day, and then it would be someone new to give shit to."

"Okay, I guess read it whenever or wherever you want. Just don't be blaming me when you get shit about it."

"I'll be fine, but I do appreciate you worrying about me. If you're worrying, then you care, which I'll take as a good sign."

I don't know what to say to that. I guess I do care about him, even if it does seem soon for such strong feelings to be developing. I feel like the time since I met Aiden has been a whirlwind. We went from perfect strangers to lovers in practically a blink of an eye, and it scares me slightly.

"You still there?" he asks.

"Yeah, sorry. Just got lost in thought for a second."

"No problem. So, what are your plans for tomorrow?" he asks, changing the subject.

"I think brunch with Avery and maybe Ellie if she wants to come with us. She spent the night at her best friend's, so Avery wasn't sure if she'd be back or want to go. After, I might try and hit up the farmers' market for some fresh produce. I also need to get some laundry and basic house cleaning done this weekend. Basically, my weekend is going to be pretty basic domestic shit that just needs to be done."

"Since you have tomorrow off, what will you do?" I ask as I unplug the tub. The water is starting to cool off more than I like, so it's time to get out.

I step out of the tub and wrap my big fluffy towel around my body. I had it hanging over my heated towel bar, so it is nice and warm.

"I'll answer your question in a second. First, I need

to know, are you getting out of the tub?"

"Yeah, the water was going cold," I tell him as I wrap my hair up in one of my hair towels.

I can hear him groan. "You're really trying to kill me tonight, aren't you?"

I just giggle. "You're the one who called me, remember?"

"Yeah, but you're the one who answered the phone while naked and in the bathtub. What kind of reaction did you expect from me when I knew you were naked on the other end of the line?" he asks.

"I guess I wasn't thinking of that," I answer honestly.

I head into my bedroom and grab some clean pajamas and underwear. I toss them on my bed and take a seat to relax in my towel while we continue to talk.

"To answer your previous question, I don't really have any specific plans. I'll sleep in as long as possible, grab some food, then maybe go for a run or jog to get in a little exercise, so my body doesn't cramp up. Other than that, just hang out with the guys. If we're feeling antsy, we might grab an Uber and head to a mall or something to go walk around, hit up a movie theater, or sometimes a golf course. Besides Ryker making dinner reservations for the evening, I don't think any other plans have been made yet."

"Do you ever get bored while on the road?" I ask.

"Not really. If there's nothing to do, I'll usually just take a nap or watch a movie in my room. I'm also not opposed to heading out by myself to find something to do, but there's usually at least one guy who also wants to head out for a few hours, so going solo doesn't happen often."

"I know you guys are a new team, but do you feel like you've created a team bond?"

"We have. Some friendships are stronger than others, but we all get along great and have one another's backs. There isn't anyone in the locker room who's toxic. I've been on a team that had a toxic player, and it made for some miserable times."

"I can't even imagine. You spend so much of your time with these people, you have to get along, or else it would be a miserable time."

"Exactly. Hey, can I let you go? The rest of the guys are getting onto the bus, and we're taking off."

"Of course, have a safe flight. Call or text me tomorrow if you aren't busy."

"I'm never too busy for you. Good night, sweetheart."

"Night," I tell him before the line goes dead.

I place my phone on the bed next to me and let my head fall back against the headboard. I can't help but let my lips turn up in a grin from the way this man makes me feel. I'm all giddy inside, butterflies taking flight from talking to him for the last half-hour.

Tiredness hits me, so I finally get up and get my pajamas on, then head back into my bathroom to comb my hair out and put it up into a twist to sleep in. I brush my teeth, then go through my nightly skincare routine before heading back to my bed, where I fall asleep to thoughts of Aiden.

CHAPTER 10
AIDEN

I slowly wake up, stretching my tired body as I look around the room. It was after two in the morning before we made it here, and I practically collapsed right into my bed. I even skipped my normal unpacking routine I was so dead on my feet.

The sheet falls down my body, tenting around my aching cock with some intensive morning wood. Thoughts of a naked Tori in the tub last night come rushing back to me, and I can't help but reach down and grip my length. She's turned my life upside down since meeting her. There's just something about her that pulls me.

I think of her supple body as I stroke my cock, my balls already tingling after just a few strokes of my hand. My mind wanders to her lips stretched around my tip, the way she'd take my cock like a good girl, down her throat.

The thought of coming down her throat has my orgasm spilling from my body; I come all over my abs.

I bask in the aftermath of my orgasm for a few minutes, wishing I was balls deep in Tori when it happened, but my hand will have to suffice for the next few days while I'm on the road.

I grab a tissue from the nightstand and wipe off my abs as best as I can before heading into the bathroom for a quick shower. I turn the water on to get warmed up before taking a quick piss. Since I didn't unpack when we got in last night, my bathroom bag isn't in here yet, so I grab it, snagging my shower items from it before stepping under the hot spray. I adjust the showerhead to a better setting and let the water relax my muscles. I stand there for a good five minutes before getting my business done and washing my hair and body off.

Once out of the shower, I towel off and pull on some jogger pants and a T-shirt. A quick look at the time, and it's already ten a.m. I probably missed breakfast, so I'll need to go in search of some food.

You up?

RYKER

Yeah, just getting moving, need to find some food.

Same. I'm about to head out and try to find some; want to come with?

Yep, meet you in the lobby in 5?

That works. I'll text the others to see if anyone else wants to come with.

Sounds good.

> Going to find some food, if you want to come, be in the lobby in 5 minutes.

I shoot off the text to our team chat, then pull up the map app on my phone to see what's around our hotel we can hit up. I find a diner only two blocks away, which sounds like the perfect location for us to go.

I head out and meet up with Ryker in the hallway. While we're waiting on the elevator, Tristan and Blake join us.

We hang out in the lobby for a few minutes, waiting on anyone else who wants to join us to do so.

"I found a diner just two blocks away," I tell the group.

"Sounds good to me," Ryker states.

"I just need a big breakfast, so sounds good to me," Blake adds.

We've waited for probably ten minutes, and my stomach is already growling, so we head out. I shoot a text to the group letting them know where we've gone in case they want to catch up.

> You awake?

My phone rings a second later, and I chuckle at the fast response. "I take that as a yes," I say as I answer.

"Yep. I would have texted back, but I'm driving," Tori says.

"Where are you headed?" I ask.

"Bunch with Avery," she answers.

"Ah, how was your morning?"

"Good. I slept in, had a cup of coffee, and now I'm ready for some food. How about you?"

"Pretty much the same. Some of the guys and I went and found a diner to grab some breakfast at. We've just been relaxing since getting back. Ryker, Jason, and I are going to head out for a run here, shortly."

"Just so you know, I hate running. Please don't ever make me do it with you."

I can't help but chuckle. "Noted. So no Thanksgiving 5K races or charity runs are in our future?"

"God, no. Thanksgiving is all about the carbs. Give me all the mashed potatoes, gravy, stuffing, pie, and a small side of turkey."

I laugh loudly. This girl is something else, but I can't get enough of her. "Got it, don't get between you and the mashed potatoes."

"Damn straight." She chuckles.

"Why don't you give me a call once you're home from your brunch and errands. We should be back from our run by then; I think we're only going for three miles, maybe five."

"Three, maybe five? How can you make it sound like it's just a jog around the neighborhood?" She laughs.

"That's nothing. I regularly run ten-plus miles, so three to five is like a nice warm-up. But it's an off day, and we don't want to overdo it."

"I'm still trying to wrap my mind around three to

five miles being a warm-up. I'd be keeled over on the ground within the first mile."

"It's why you start small and build up your endurance. I didn't start out running this much, but over time I was able to build my stamina up."

"You do have some impressive stamina," she murmurs.

"You noticed that, did you?" I smirk.

"Um, yeah. I can tell you, without a doubt, you've lasted longer than any other man I've been with."

"As much as I don't want to think about the men who have come before me, I'll take the compliment," I chuckle.

"As you should; you've ruined me for anyone else."

"Good, because I'm claiming you as mine."

"Way to be a caveman," she retorts.

"I don't share, Tori. I thought I made that clear already."

"I wasn't implying any sharing would happen; I'm just, never mind, let's not go there right now."

I know what she's doing. She's thinking I'll move on. Little does she know, I don't plan on going anywhere.

"All right, we can drop it. But let me reiterate, I don't plan on going anywhere."

"Okay," she concedes.

"Call me later?" I state, but also try and state it more as a question, so she doesn't feel like I'm demanding it.

"Yeah, I'll call once I'm back home this afternoon. What time are you guys going to dinner?"

"Reservations are at seven; I think we have to leave

the hotel around five thirty since it's in New York City and traffic can be a bitch."

"Okay, that's only, like, two thirty here, so I'll text if it's after, by the time I get home, to see if you're free."

"Sounds good, babe. Have a fun time with Avery."

"We always have a good time." She chuckles.

"Don't get into too much trouble. Ryker and I are across the country and can't just come down and bail the two of you out." I laugh.

"Ha ha." She pretends to laugh at my statement. "I'd like to make it known, I've never been arrested. Hell, I've never even gotten a speeding ticket. I'm a good girl."

"A good girl," I repeat. "Maybe in the boardroom, but in the bedroom, you're quite the little vixen."

"Only for you," she retorts.

"Fuck, you keep talking like that, and I'm going to go hard, right now. I've already rubbed one out today thinking of you," I tell her.

"You did?"

"Fuck yes. I woke up and couldn't get the thoughts of you in the tub last night out of my mind. Had my cock so hard and ready to sink inside you. I had to settle with my hand and coming all over my abs."

"I might have pulled out bob to take care of business this morning," she admits.

"Bob?" I ask, quirking a brow, even though she can't see me.

"Bob, battery-operated-boyfriend," she says, spelling it out for me.

"Oh, was he as good as me?"

"You're incorrigible." She laughs. "He gets the job done, but nothing like the real thing."

"Good. Now go before I convince you into some phone sex."

"I'm driving, remember?" She laughs. "Not really feasible, at the moment."

I grumble, knowing she's right. "Are you almost to your destination?" I ask, changing the subject and hoping my hard-on goes away.

"Yep, just waiting for the light to flip so I can turn into the parking lot."

"Okay, have fun, and I'll talk to you later."

"Have a good run," she says before the line goes silent.

I change into my running clothes, thankful my hard-on is gone. That wouldn't have been fun to run with, painful, actually.

> Are you guys ready to hit the pavement?

JASON

Yep, I just need to put my shoes on, and I'm good.

RYKER

Same

> I'll see you in the hallway then. I've got a route mapped out, either a three mile or five.

JASON

I vote for three.

RYKER

I'm good with either.

I'm also good with either, so three it is.

I grab my water bottle that has a hand strap and fill it up before heading out to the hallway to wait for the guys.

We hit the pavement, falling into an easy pace as we make our way through the route I made for us. Thankfully, the area we're staying in has a decent trail system, so it made it easy to map out.

"You guys kicked my ass," Jason says once we return to the hotel. He's bent over, sucking in deep breaths as he tries to fill his lungs with oxygen.

"I thought you youngins were supposed to be in better shape than us older guys?" I tease him.

"Fuck off," he retorts. "I swear, you fuckers purposely pushed it the last mile."

"Maybe." I chuckle. "Had to see what you had in you."

"Well, now you know," he says, and I worry he might puke all over the sidewalk.

"We'll go easy on you next time." Ryker chuckles.

"You'd better, or I won't run with you fuckers again. That was brutal," he states as he finally catches his breath and starts to stand back up.

"Just think of the stamina it will build. I'm sure Olivia will appreciate it." Ryker smirks.

"She's perfectly happy with my stamina," he quips. "Never been a complaint fall from her lips with my bedroom skills."

"Just making sure, rookie. Wouldn't want to get a bad rep in bed."

"You worry about your own woman, and I'll worry about mine, deal?"

"Deal." I laugh.

CHAPTER 11
TORI

"Can I ask you a question?" I say to Avery as we both eat away at our brunch. It is just the two of us this morning; Ellie is staying with her friend for the entire day.

"Always," she says, giving me a look like why did you even ask.

"When you and Ryker first got together, did you have apprehension about starting a relationship with a professional athlete?"

"A little bit, but it wasn't so bad. I saw firsthand how devoted he was to Ellie, and realized his devotion would roll over into other areas of his life. I also never really got the playboy vibe from him, so that notion never really was a worry of mine. What worries you about being with Aiden?"

"There isn't anything specific I can put my finger on. I think I'm just more worried about falling for him, and then my heart being broken when he moves on to a supermodel or someone younger than me."

"I know you haven't known each other long, but do you really think he's that kind of guy?"

"After getting to know him, I have no reason to believe that would happen, but look at all the women out there who think they have the perfect life, and boom, their husbands leave them after twenty years for someone half their age."

"You can't hold what other men do to their wives against other men. Just because one is that way doesn't mean Aiden will be."

"I know; I just need to let go and let what's going to happen between us happen."

"I think he's a great guy. He's always been respectful and nice when I've been around him. Just enjoy it. If it doesn't work out, at least you tried and got some amazing orgasms out of the deal. If it does, then you'll be happy for the rest of your life and be spoiled with those orgasms until you die."

"I like the way you think." I chuckle and pick up my mimosa to click against Avery's.

We talk and laugh as we enjoy our brunch. It's always a good time when we get together. Avery and I are like long-lost sisters. I don't know what I'd do without her in my life. She often keeps me grounded and is the voice of reason I often need.

"Want to do dinner sometime this week?" Avery asks as we wait for our server to return with our cards.

"Sure, maybe Tuesday?" I'm not sure what my schedule looks like this week I know it isn't super busy since I'm taking off Thursday and Friday, but it also means if anything important comes up, I need to take care of it before then.

"We can make it a taco and margarita night?" I suggest.

"You know it! Ellie loves tacos, so she'll be all over it."

"Sounds like a girls' night, then. I'll pick up a taco kit, and you supply the margs. Sound good?"

"Works for me. Should we plan on six?" Avery asks.

"Yep, if I can get out any earlier and get the food picked up, I'll let you know."

"We'll be there; Ellie gets home by three."

"I don't think it will be before five thirty, but you never know."

"Six is perfect, plus, we can watch the game that night, as well," Avery reminds me.

"It's like it was meant to be." I chuckle as we head outside to the parking lot. We stop on the curb and give each other a big hug. "Thanks for meeting me today."

"Of course! You know I don't turn down brunch. I've got to go grocery shopping now and back home to get some cleaning done."

"Same." I laugh at our identical days.

"I swear, we have the same brain some days." Avery laughs as we part ways.

I stop at the farmers' market and browse the booths. It is more crafters selling their handmade items than farmers these days, but I still enjoy walking around and checking everything out. I pick up some fruit and vegetables for some salads and smoothies this week before stopping at the grocery store for a few other items I need before heading home.

I get the food all put away, then toss in my first load of laundry. I check the time, and it's already three, so I'm sure Aiden is already gone for their dinner reservation, but I text him anyways since I said I would.

> I'm home and will be all night, so call whenever you're free.

The three little dots start bouncing almost immediately, so I wait for his reply to pop up.

AIDEN

In the Uber to dinner, I'll call once we're back at the hotel, it will be a few hours, but I won't forget.

> No rush, enjoy your dinner. I'm just about to start cleaning.

Will do; how was brunch?

> So good, both the food and the company.

Glad you enjoyed yourself.

> Always, have a good time at dinner!

Sure thing. Talk soon.

I pull up my music app and pick an upbeat station to blast and keep me motivated as I clean my condo. Once I have my phone paired to the speakers I have in all the rooms, I get to work, tackling it all. Dusting, sweeping, mopping, vacuuming. I scrub the toilet and shower and even manage to change the sheets on my bed, all before collapsing on the couch a few hours later. I've worked up quite the appetite after all that work but don't feel like cooking. I scan through one of the food delivery apps on my phone, finally settling on a wrap from a small restaurant not far away from my condo, so hopefully, it won't be a super long wait for my food to arrive. I splurge and add on their strawberry cheese-cake, as it is so good.

Once I submit my order, it estimates it will be forty-five minutes until it will arrive, so I take the time to go shower off. I'm all sweaty and grimy from cleaning all afternoon. I put on some yoga pants and a loose-fitting T-shirt and call it a night. I'm not going anywhere, nor do I have anyone to impress with the way I look tonight. It's the perfect night to pick a show, and binge watch it.

I pick a true crime show I haven't watched yet and settle in for the night. My food arrives about ten minutes into the first episode, which scares the crap out of me when the phone rings and the delivery girl needs in.

"Thank you," I tell her as I accept the bag. I hand her an additional cash tip on top of what I gave in the app. I remember being a young and broke college student, not that it is what she is, but I know every tip counts when you're a delivery person.

"Have a good night," she tells me before turning and heading out.

I take my food inside and plop back down on the

couch, turning the episode back on. I get sucked into the show, eating while I watch. The wrap was so good and filled me right up. I put the cheesecake in the fridge for later. I'm too stuffed to eat it now.

I'm on my third episode when my phone rings; I check the screen and see Aiden and my picture filling it, and I can't help but smile that he's FaceTiming me.

"Hey," I answer as I sink back into the couch. I've paused my show, so I don't miss anything while talking to him.

"Hey, yourself. You look comfortable, what are you doing?"

"Just binging a show and having a relaxing night after my busy day."

"Did you get everything done you wanted?" he asks. It looks like he's on his hotel bed, propped up against the headboard.

"I did. I put on some music and got to work. Got everything done in around three hours and then collapsed on the couch. I ordered in some dinner and have just been relaxing since."

"Sounds like the perfect night."

"It was, how was your dinner?"

"Great, I'm still stuffed."

"Did you guys just go to dinner?"

"Yep, everyone wanted to get back so we could get a good night's sleep under us before the game tomorrow. With it being a Sunday game, we're playing an afternoon game, so our game day routine will be thrown off."

"That sucks."

"Eh, we're used to it. Sunday games tend to be earlier. Makes it easier for the fans to attend, but not be out late with work or school the next day."

"I can appreciate it, but it's at your expense."

"Like I said, we're used to it."

"What time is it at? I'll try and be home to watch it."

"It's a five-o'clock puck drop here, so two back home."

"Shouldn't be an issue; I didn't plan on going anywhere tomorrow, as of now."

"Just a lazy day tomorrow, then?" he asks.

"Yep. I might go to a yoga class, but other than that, I don't have any plans."

"Mmm, I bet you look hot in a yoga outfit."

"You are so bad." I laugh.

"Can't blame a man for thinking of his woman in sexy workout clothes. Ones I'm guessing hug every curve. Dammit, I'm getting hard just thinking about it."

"I swear, I could breathe around you, and it would make you hard."

"Pretty much," he agrees, scratching at the scruff on his face. His long hair falling to the side of his face makes me wish he was here and I could run my hands through the soft locks. "What is that look for?" he asks, obviously catching me zoning out and wishing we were in the same room.

"What look?" I ask, trying to play it off.

"The one where you were just eye fucking me."

"I don't know what you are talking about." I smirk.

"Hmm, I guess if you don't want to tell me, I'll just have to let my imagination go to work."

"And what does your imagination think I was thinking about?" I ask, curious what he's going to say.

"Well, since you started eye fucking me when I was scratching my beard, I think you were imagining me between your thighs. Eating your pussy until you come all over my face multiple times. Your fingers sliding through my hair, holding me right where you want me as it starts to feel so good you can't control yourself from screaming out my name."

I can feel my body flushing, my clit tingling as his words work me up. It is a little scary how accurate his imagination is to what I was thinking about.

"I'll take your silence as a good sign." He winks at me. "Should I continue?" he asks.

"Um," I stammer, not sure what to tell him.

"Do I have you all hot and bothered?" he asks, and the half smile on his face is smug and sexy all at once.

"Yes, my clit is throbbing," I tell him honestly.

"Then reach down and play with it, baby."

I look all around my condo, for what, I don't know.

"You can do it, Tori, let me help you come," he purrs.

"I don't know, Aiden," I tell him.

"You don't have to show me what you're doing if it makes you uncomfortable. Just let my voice bring you to orgasm."

"Let me move to my bed," I tell him, taking the leap to try something new with him. If I'm going to go all in with this relationship, I need to be open to new experiences.

"That's my good girl," he soothes.

I quickly move to my room and prop the phone up on my nightstand as I strip off my clothes. "You are alone with no chance of any of your teammates walking in, correct?" I ask, suddenly worried.

"No chance in hell," he states. "We each get our own room, and no one else has a key."

"Okay," I say and pick up the phone again, now allowing him to see I've stripped out of my clothes.

"Fuuuuck," he growls. "You are a fucking goddess. Give me a second, and I'll join you in being naked," he says, but sets his phone so I can see him strip out of his clothes. When he removes his shirt, his inked skin comes into view. I've enjoyed tracing all the ink lines on his torso and right arm.

I lie down on the bed while he's stripping, trying to figure out a comfortable position that allows me to still see him but not have to hold the phone. I decided to grab my vibrator out of the bedside drawer, as I usually can't make myself come without it. I put it out of view of the camera, not sure what Aiden will think of me using it while we're on the phone together.

"Are you still good?" he asks as he props himself up on the bed. He's lazily stroking his cock, and I'm mesmerized by the sight of it.

I must not answer quick enough, as he laughs. "Tori, you good?"

"Yeah," I stammer, and bring my eyes up to meet his through the camera.

"It's okay, baby. You can watch my cock all you want."

"I honestly don't know what to look at," I tell him.

"You look wherever you want. Reach down and circle your clit with your fingers, and play with your nipples with the other," he instructs as he continues to stroke his cock.

My eyes close as I do as he says. Trying to not think about what I look like to him over the video.

"So fucking hot," he grits. "That's it, baby. Now, slide those fingers down and inside your pussy."

I know it isn't going to work for me, so I reach over and grab my vibrator. I slide it through my folds, before inserting it inside me. I press the button, turning it on to the lowest speed.

"Fucking hell, you're a vixen," he says as he watches me fuck myself with the vibrator. I click the button again, turning the speed up a notch, as well as turning on the part that flicks my clit.

"Aiden," I moan. "I'm close," I warn him.

"Me too, baby. Keep fucking yourself. You look so gorgeous. I can't wait to eat you up when I get home Thursday morning."

"Yes!" I cry out, my orgasm barreling through me. "I'm coming," I tell him, like he can't tell from my cries.

"That's my good girl," he praises. "Now, open your eyes and watch what you do to me," he says, and I do as he says. It's only seconds later when he's calling my name out and coming all over his abs. It's incredibly hot. Hotter than I ever imagined phone or video sex would be. I don't know what my hesitation was about it, but this put my nerves at ease. "You'll have to show me where you keep that stored. I might have to use it on you." He smirks.

"Really? Using it wouldn't make you uncomfortable?"

"Babe, a real man isn't going to be insecure about a vibrator. If it makes you feel good and helps you come, then why should I give two shits if you have one or if we use it during foreplay?"

"My past boyfriends have all hated the fact I had one and would use it on myself."

"That's because they were insecure and probably didn't even know how to find your clit. Best yet, make you come multiple times in a night."

"You hit that nail on the head," I tell him.

"Fucking bastards. Deserve to have their dicks chopped off," he mutters, and I can't help but laugh.

"Thanks for the laugh," I tell him. I shift so I can pull my sheet up over me, as I'm starting to get chilly. "Will you sleep better now?" I ask him.

"Hopefully, as long as the mental images of you making yourself come don't keep me up and in a perpetual state of hardness."

"Oh my god, please don't tell me that can happen."

"I don't know, never had it happen, but the images are now burned into my mind will always be kept there for when I need to rub one out."

I laugh and shake my head at him. It's moments like this that make me even more giddy about him and what's brewing between the two of us. "I guess I should take it as a compliment you'd want to think of me while pleasuring yourself."

"I'd think of no one else."

"Really? Not some hot model or some porn on your phone?"

"Maybe in the past, but why would I turn to those now when I've got something even better?"

"I don't know how to answer that," I tell him honestly. This man just keeps surprising me.

"Don't get me wrong, porn comes in handy sometimes, but it isn't the end all be all for getting my rocks off. I could take it or leave it, to be honest with you. I'd much rather call you up and talk you through an orgasm than watching some porn stars going at it. Watching you come is becoming my favorite thing to experience."

"I'm sure it's super awkward."

"Not at all; it's beautiful, sensual, and turns me on."

"You're such a sweet talker," I tell him. "I like how much you stroke my ego."

"Not trying to stroke your ego, just telling you how it is. I wish you could see yourself through my eyes. I think you're beautiful. I know it's a default thought for most women to not think of themselves as beautiful. They always see flaws, but as a man, I don't see those. I see your caring personality, your assertiveness, compassion, and fierce protectiveness when it comes to your friends or family. All of those attributes just add to your natural beauty. You might look at your curves as a bad thing, but I look at them as a woman who's confident in her skin. Someone who isn't afraid to feed her body with good food, isn't obsessed with the gym or the number on the scale. I don't want a woman I have to worry I'm going to break in half when I fuck her hard. I want a woman I can hold on to. There's nothing wrong with having a little cushion for the pushing." He winks, and I think I fall in love with him in this instant. If this feeling isn't love, I don't know what it is.

I laugh at his statement. "I can't believe you just said that last part." I laugh some more. "But thank you for the rest. It makes me feel good you think so highly of me. I can only hope I don't let you down."

"I don't think that's going to happen," he states as he tries to hide a yawn behind his hand.

"I should let you get to bed. It looks like you're exhausted."

His eyes flick away from the camera. "Yeah, it's getting late here," he says, bringing his eyes back to mine. "I need a good night's sleep since I won't get much of an afternoon nap tomorrow."

"With an early puck drop, do you even try taking one?"

"Sometimes. I won't go to any morning skate, probably won't even leave the hotel until I get on the bus for the ride over for the game. Just hang out here, maybe do a mile or so on the treadmill or elliptical in the hotel's gym to get my blood flowing, then lay down by noon for ninety minutes or so."

"Okay, call or text when you're free. I don't want to call you and accidentally wake you up or keep you from falling asleep."

"A call from you would never be a bother," he says, but I'm already shaking my head no.

"You need your sleep, and you need to keep to your routine. I don't need anyone blaming me because something changes in your routine that affects your play. Nope, not happening," I insist.

He grumbles but eventually agrees. "Fine, I'll call you before my nap; how's that?"

"Works for me," I tell him. After my busy afternoon, food, and the orgasm I've had, I'm suddenly feeling tired myself. "I could fall right to sleep; I'm feeling so relaxed."

"Sounds like I did my job, then; get some sleep, and we'll talk tomorrow," Aiden says before we disconnect the video call.

CHAPTER 12
AIDEN

THIS ROAD TRIP CAN'T END FAST ENOUGH. I'M READY TO BE back in my condo or Tori's; I'm not picky. Wherever she's at, I'm content with. I just need her in my arms or under me; hell, I'll even settle with her on top. I just need to sink inside her tight heat and lose myself.

The four-game road trip ends with the one win in a shootout, two losses, and a final win in regulation.

Coach walks into the locker room, his interview obviously done after tonight's hard-fought win. "Nice work out there tonight, men. I'm proud of how you fought until the last seconds of the game to pull out the win. We knew this season wasn't going to be easy, being the newest team in the league, so every win we get is a positive. I can't say enough about the effort every single one of you are putting in on and off the ice to build the camaraderie needed to pull off a winning season. Tonight's player of the game is Blake. The shots he faced tonight were crazy, but his efforts kept us in the game." Coach finishes his speech, and Ryker hands

Blake the belt we pass from guy to guy each game as the player of the game award.

Everyone cheers, congratulating him on the job well done.

Once we're all done, everyone focuses on getting stripped from their gear, showered, dressed, and on the bus as soon as possible. We all want to get home, and we know that the faster we get out of here, the sooner we head home.

I texted Tori the door code to my place, yesterday, hoping she'd use it and be waiting in my bed when I return. She wouldn't commit to it the last I talked to her, so my anticipation is high when I unlock my door.

I drop my suitcase just inside the foyer, toss my keys on the counter, and head for my bedroom. I stay as quiet as possible, not wanting to wake her if she is in my bed. I use the light from my cell to illuminate the way.

The most beautiful sight greets me when I enter the bedroom. Her body curled up, hair flowing across the pillow as she peacefully sleeps.

I quietly head for the bathroom, closing the door behind me before turning on any lights. I quickly do my business, wash my hands, and brush my teeth before turning the light back off and heading back into the room. I strip down to my boxers and slide into bed next to Tori. I run a hand down her body and find her completely naked. My cock hardens, and the need to be inside her is so incredibly strong, I can't just roll over.

I slide a hand down, finding her clit. I rub circles around it as I whisper in her ear. "Tori, baby, I'm home," I state as she starts to stir, her body opening to me as she enjoys the pressure on her clit.

"Aiden," she murmurs, "what time is it?"

"About two thirty," I tell her as I start to kiss along her jaw.

"So early," she says sleepily. I roll away, only long enough to remove my boxers. I return to her, sliding down her body, kissing as I go. I need her taste on my tongue, so I press on, not taking much time to suck on her pert nipples. I can come back to them, but for now, I've got a one-track mind, and that's for my mouth to be on her pussy.

I slide my cheeks along the inside of her thighs, tickling her with my facial hair like we talked about while I was gone. I suck her clit into my mouth, flicking it with my tongue as she squirms on the bed.

"Aiden." She moans, and I know she's close. I slide two fingers inside, her walls already clenching around them as I pump in and out. Her hands slide into my hair, nails digging into my scalp as she holds my head still and starts to roll her hips just how she wants me. I let her take control, as there's nothing sexier than a woman taking control of her own pleasure.

Her body goes rigid, thighs clamping around my head as she comes all over my hand and face. I lap at her juices, loving I'm the one to make her fall over the cliff like this.

Once Tori's body has gone limp, I pull my fingers from inside her, give her clit one last suckle, which has her body arching again as another small orgasm rolls through her. I smile against her, then lightly kiss her body as I slide back up. I stop at her tits, suckling at each of her nipples as she basks in the afterglow of her orgasms.

"That was one hell of a welcome home," she says, pulling my attention away from her tits.

"Best way to find you, that's for sure," I tell her as I push up higher and capture her lips with mine. Our tongues tangle as we devour one another. Tori grips my length, stroking me as we make out.

"Fuck, you feel good," I tell her when we break apart.

"Lie back," she instructs. I do as she asks, wondering what she's going to do next.

I watch as she slides down the bed, her fist still wrapped around my cock. She licks at my tip, and I almost come just from the touch of her tongue.

"God damn," I grit as I grind my teeth together to hold back from coming way too fucking soon.

"You like?" she asks, her eyes flying to meet mine before she sucks my entire length into her mouth, stopping only when I hit the back of her throat, and she chokes on my tip. She pulls back, popping my tip out of her mouth as her hand works my shaft.

"You're such a good girl, taking all of my cock like this," I praise her.

She slides my length back into her mouth, this time bobbing up and down, her hand covering the portion not in her mouth. She sucks me all the way in again, this time anticipating my tip hitting the back of her throat, so she's ready. I feel the muscles of her throat contract around my tip, and I almost lose control. I have to fight the urge to thrust up and come down the back of her throat. Maybe next time; tonight, I want to come while buried deep inside her pussy.

I tap her cheek. "I need inside you."

She takes me out of her mouth, still stroking me. "You were inside me," she says, smiling as her mouth heads back for my tip.

"I need inside your pussy," I state, making my intentions clear.

I take quick action, rolling us over, pinning Tori underneath me. I slide my cock through her folds, teasing her clit with my tip.

"Need you inside me," she moans.

"Give me a second," I tell her as I reach for the condoms in my nightstand. I quickly rip the packet open and roll it down my length. As soon as I have it secured, I'm nudging myself against her opening and sinking in, not stopping until my balls slap against her ass.

"Holy shit," she moans.

"So fucking good," I whisper into her ear. I pull out, thrusting back in. I find a quick and punishing rhythm that has us both breathing hard as our sweaty bodies slap together.

"I'm going to come," Tori says. I didn't need her words to know she's close. I can tell by the way her pussy grips my cock like it's never letting go. I fight through the tightness, not wanting to lose either of our pent up orgasms. I keep pumping my hips, adjusting slightly so I can slip a hand between us, finding her clit. As soon as I press against her bundle of nerves, she flies over the cliff, her orgasm taking control as her body shakes with the intensity. She pulls me right over the edge of my own, and I come so hard, I'm worried I might have broke the condom with the force of my orgasm.

I collapse down, trying hard not to put too much of my weight directly onto Tori. I don't have the strength to move for a minute or so, but as soon as I do, I roll off of her, taking her with me.

"That was…" she starts to say.

"The best welcome home ever," I finish for her, and she lightly chuckles.

"That works, but I was going to say the best I've ever had. I don't think I've ever had an orgasm so powerful before."

Knowing I'm the best she's ever had, has me floating on cloud fucking nine. "Same, baby," I tell her as I push her hair from her face and drop a chaste kiss to her lips. The problem is, things don't stay chaste between us. We both crave one another on a deeper level, and it shows by the way we're just drawn to each other.

We lazily make out for a few minutes, but I pull back when I feel myself start to go soft. I want to clean up and take care of the condom before we end up with a mess on the sheets. "I'll be right back, let me take care of the condom. Do you need anything while I'm up?" I ask before dropping a kiss to the tip of her nose.

"Can you bring me a glass of water?" she asks.

"Of course, anything else?"

"No, I'll clean up once you're done in the bathroom."

"You can go first," I tell her. "Or just come in with me. Want to take a shower before we climb back into bed?" I ask, cocking an eyebrow in question.

"Something tells me a shower wouldn't make us clean, but rather dirtier, if it's even possible."

"Just think, I could pin you against the tile wall, sink in this tight pussy, or maybe take you from behind, your hands spread on the wall, trying to keep yourself steady as I pound you from behind. Shit, baby, I'm already getting hard thinking of all the ways I could take you in the shower."

"I swear, you have the rebound time of a sixteen-year-old."

"Hell no, when I was sixteen, I didn't have this kind of rebound, trust me."

We stare at each other, waiting for someone to make the first move on what's going to happen next. I finally stand up, slide the used condom off, and tie it before tossing it into my trash can. I hold a hand out for Tori to take. "Come with me?" I ask.

She slips her hand into mine, and I bring our clasped hands up to my lips, kissing the back of her hand. I lead her into the bathroom, turning on only the accent lights, rather than the big bright main ones. It keeps it intimate in here, which I think will come in handy. I pull out a couple of clean towels from the cabinet and hang them over the towel rod, then reach in and turn the water on.

"I'll go grab you that glass of ice water and meet

you back here," I tell her before stepping out of the bathroom. I figured I'd give her a few minutes of privacy in case she needs to use the bathroom and doesn't want me in there while she does.

I come back into the bathroom and find her under the spray of water. I stand there, just watching as she relaxes under the water, the glass shower enclosure giving me full access to her beautiful body on display.

"Are you going to join me or just stand there like a peeping Tom?" she asks, and I can hear the humor in her question.

"Just enjoying the view," I tell her as I step inside and join her. I turn on the second showerhead, covering both of us with hot water.

We both just stand there, taking each other in as we face one another.

"What are you thinking?" I finally ask, curious as to what is going on in that mind of hers.

She purses her lips, thinking before she answers. "Trying to decide what way I want you to fuck me in the shower, first," she says. My chin about hits the floor, as that wasn't what I thought she'd be thinking about. I thought she might tell me not tonight, since we've already rocked each other's world in bed.

"While there can only be one first, it doesn't mean we can't try both before I let you come," I tell her as I pick her up, backing her against the tile wall. Her legs wrap around my waist, putting her in the perfect position for my cock to side through her folds.

She moves her hips slightly, coating her juices on my tip. "Fuck me, Aiden," she says as serious as can be.

"Shit," I curse, my head falling back as I realize I forgot to bring condoms into the shower with us.

"What?" she asks, concern lacing her voice.

"I forgot the condoms," I tell her as I move to set her down so I can go grab them.

"It's okay. I'm on the pill, so we're good if you're okay with it," she tells me, and I'm floored she'd have so much confidence in me to have unprotected sex with her.

"You sure? I'm clean. I have to get tested before the start of each season as part of my physical, but I'd understand if you wanted me to go grab one. I don't ever go without," I try and assure her.

Tori cups my face, pulling me in for a quick kiss. "I wouldn't have suggested it if I wasn't." She pauses, pulling back enough so we can make better eye contact.

I don't hesitate, shifting her body so I can thrust up and into her.

The growl that leaves my lips as I slide inside her with nothing between us is guttural. I've never felt anything like this, and I can only believe it's because this is happening with Tori. "I'm just warning you now; I'm not going to last long without a condom," I say between gritted teeth. My body pumps into hers at a punishing pace.

"Not going to last, either; you feel so good," she tells me as she holds firm to my face.

Our eye contact never breaks. It's almost as if we're seeing past the outside and into one another's souls as we crash over the edge together. My body pulses hard, emptying every last drop of cum it can muster into her.

If she wasn't on birth control, I don't see how that wouldn't have made her pregnant. The fleeting thought has me thinking of the future and her round with our babies. I shake my head, needing to let those thoughts stay idle for a few years. No need to rush things or scare her away with my thoughts.

Once we've both stopped convulsing, I slip from inside her and set her down, making sure she's stable before I let go of her.

"Feeling okay?" I ask a minute later. We're both in a sleepy, post-sex haze.

"Feeling perfect." She sighs. "And tired, oh so tired."

"Let's get out of here and back to bed. I promise not to attack you again until at least morning time," I tell her before we both step out of the shower. We quickly dry off and slip back into bed together. I pull her into my arms, and we both quickly settle in and drift off to sleep. My body is sated and ready for a good eight hours, minimum.

CHAPTER 13
TORI

Two Months Later

I sit at the conference table, surrounded by my team. We're going over the final details before we board a plane tomorrow to fly out east and meet up with the band we'll be going on tour with for the next two weeks. The record label was able to secure us a bus to stay with everyone else, rather than fly from city to city or drive ourselves in a rental car and then have to stay in hotels every night. Other than being away from Aiden and Avery for that time, I'm looking forward to the experience.

"Any last minute changes I need to be aware of?" I ask everyone at large.

Rebecca lifts her hand, noting she's bringing something to our attention. "We had one change for the tour's final stop; the venue had issues with the merchandise stand being outside the venue, then concertgoers bringing in their items through security.

They said it would slow down the flow and make it harder for them to spot prohibited items. I got them to compromise by allowing us to put up a temporary fence around the fan experience area so people can go through security before entering. Their tickets won't be scanned until they enter the actual building; that way, if someone wants to come and do the fan experience and doesn't have a ticket, they still can. Once they pass the security checkpoint, they won't have to go through security again. It will also allow people to take their items back to their cars if they don't want to hold on to it while in the concert."

"Good work coming up with the solution. We can have it in our back pocket to suggest to any other venues who might have the same concerns or issues," I tell Rebecca.

"Thank you; I thought it was a good compromise."

"All right, anyone else have anything to add?" I ask once more.

All four of them shake their heads no, so that's my cue we're as prepared as we're going to be. "Great, I want everyone to take the rest of the day off. Go spend some time with your families, do the last-minute packing, whatever it is you need to get done. I'll see you all at the airport tomorrow morning at nine."

"Thanks, Tori," Quinn says, followed by the others.

"Have a great night," I call out as they all file out of the conference room. I head for my boss's office, wanting to check in before I also hit the road to get some things done before morning.

"Hey, Tori," Willow greets me. She's George's daughter-in-law and personal receptionist.

"Hi, Willow. How are you doing today?" I ask. Her very swollen belly causes her to sit back from her desk. She's still a couple of months from having a set of twins, but it looks like she's ready to have them today.

"Tired. These babies think two a.m. is the perfect time to be boxing each other and keeping me awake for hours at a time."

"I'm sorry, that sounds miserable." I grimace, not sure how women make it through pregnancies.

"Eh, it will be worth it once they're here. I just have to make it a few more weeks, and it can happen."

"I hope that husband of yours is taking good care of you," I tell her.

"Oh, don't worry, he's been great. He is always helping me with things I can't do anymore, like putting my socks or shoes on. I made him shave my legs the other day, as well. Plus, an endless number of back, leg, and feet massages. He got me into this; he can deal with all the consequences that come with knocking me up." She laughs.

"Glad to hear. Hey, is George in and available?" I ask her, getting to why I really wandered this way.

"He is; go on in." She motions to his propped open door.

One of the things I love about this label is it is so unlike most others. We're all one big family around here. It's not everyone against each other. We're not cutthroat like most in this business. We want to see each other succeed.

"Tori," George bellows my name as I enter his office. I take the chair across from him. "How are things going?" he asks.

"Great," I tell him. "I just had a final meeting with my team before we fly out tomorrow. I gave them the rest of the day off to go spend time with family or do any last-minute things they need to do before leaving," I tell him.

"Good, good. I like that you are looking after them. It makes you a good leader," he compliments me, and I can't help but smile at his words.

"Thank you, Sir. I learned from the best," I tell him.

"I hope you're going to follow your own advice and head out, yourself." He smiles kindly at me.

"I will; I just wanted to check in with you, first."

"Thank you for that. Keep me posted on how things go. If you need anything, you know how to find me. And I mean it. I don't care how big or little the problem is. If you need something, you call."

"Thank you, Sir; I'll send updates after each show with how things are going and any changes I think we need to implement."

"Good, good," he states. "I'm confident in your ability to lead your team, plus represent my company. I wouldn't have promoted you if I didn't have that confidence. You've really proved yourself this past year. Before you take off, I wanted to give you this," he tells me as he slides a sealed envelope across the desk to me. I take it and slip my finger under the closed flap, then pull the papers out.

George stays quiet as I read the paper; it's a review

stating all the positives I've brought to the company. I reach the last paragraph and gasp as I read it.

> *Tori, your glowing review will not come without reward. Effective today, your yearly salary will increase to two-hundred-and-fifty-thousand dollars per year. You will also be eligible for a thirty percent yearly bonus, calculated and paid out each December based on company-wide profits. A full detail on how this is calculated will be provided to you separately from this letter. We are also increasing your company match for your retirement account from five to ten percent. We appreciate your dedication to our company and feel you more than deserve this raise.*
>
> *Bravo on a job well done!*
>
> *~ George*

I look up at George, tears already sliding down my cheeks. "I don't even know what to say but thank you."

"We are the ones that need to thank you, and we hope you realize just how important to our organization you are. We don't ever want to lose you as an asset. I hope this raise shows just how important we see you. Keep up the impeccable work, and I can assure you, more reviews like the one in your hands will come your way."

"I promise to never let you down; thank you," I tell him again. I don't think the shock of receiving this large of a pay raise will really sink in for a long time. I can't wait to get out of here and call Aiden. I know a quarter of a million dollars a year is nothing compared to the contract he has, but it is still an incredible milestone in my career.

"I know you won't. That's why I put you in your position. Now, go, get out of here. Go celebrate your good news with your boyfriend and best friend or whomever it is you want to share the good news with. I look forward to your first report out on the road," he says, and stands as I do, too.

He rounds his desk and gives me a big hug before I can leave his office.

"Oh, and just so you know, when you return from this trip, Reese will be flying into town. She's personally asked to work directly with you regarding her upcoming tour. Said she'd only agree to one if you're in charge." George winks at me. He knows how much I love working with Reese Blackwood. She's probably my favorite artist on our roster, and that's saying something.

I head back to my office, still floating on cloud nine as I collect my things, making sure I'm not forgetting anything I might need on the road. I've got my laptop all packed up in my shoulder bag, along with every-thing I might need to set up a mini office in the bus. Travel printer, paper, pens, sticky notes, you name it, we probably have it in a box or can easily head to a store in any one of the cities we'll be in to grab it.

I head for a liquor store. News like I received today calls for some celebrating. I grab a bottle of champagne, then make my way to Aiden's condo. We spend practi-cally every night he's in town together, these days, and split time between our respective places. I do love his condo; it has the most amazing view and is closer to my office when it comes to my commute.

"Hey, babe, you're home early," Aiden greets as I walk in. He's in the kitchen making himself some lunch. He's got an off day, as they just returned last night from a road trip. I purposely planned for my team not to leave until tomorrow so we could have a little time together before I had to leave. Unfortunately, when I return, he'll have just left for a four-day road trip, so it will be even longer before we see one another.

"I sent my team home after our morning meeting and gave them the rest of the day off," I tell him, holding back my exciting news.

"How nice of you; what's the champagne for? Are we celebrating tonight?" he asks, a brow quirked in question.

"After I sent everyone home, I went and met with George. He gave me this," I tell him and hand him the letter. I wait as patiently as I can while he reads it, his eyes bulging when he reaches the last paragraph.

"Holy shit, babe, this is amazing. Congratulations!" Aiden exclaims as he puts the letter down on the counter and picks me up, spinning me in a circle before setting me back down and crashing his lips to mine. "I'm so fucking proud of you," he says against my lips.

"Thank you; I was so shocked; I was practically speechless when I read the letter," I tell him, recounting my meeting.

"I bet you were. This calls for more than a bottle of champagne; this calls for a night out. You invite whoever you want, and I'll get us reservations somewhere nice."

"Are you sure? I know you were looking forward to a night in with just the two of us before we're apart for a few weeks."

"Don't worry, babe, I can still ravish you tonight. Hell, we've got a few hours before dinnertime. I'm sure I can fit in at least three, maybe four orgasms in that amount of time." He winks and smacks my ass.

I just shake my head and laugh at his antics. "You're something else. You know that?" I tell him.

"You know you love me," he says, and then stops. We haven't yet broached the sentiment of telling one another we love each other. I've felt the feeling for a while now; I've just been too chicken to actually let the words fall from my mouth. I felt like if I put them out there, the universe would take him away from me and shatter my heart. "Please don't freak out," he tries to overcorrect.

"No, you're right, I do love you," I say, not stopping the smile filling my face. I love this man, and I'm more than ready to let him know so.

He pulls me back into his arms, sliding his hands up my body until he's cupping my cheeks. "That's good because I'm in love with you. So fucking much." He kisses me hard, our tongues dueling as we seal our sentiments with a kiss.

"All right, I've invited Ryker and Avery, and my parents, so we'll need reservations for six of us," I tell Aiden an hour later. It took me a little bit to hear back from everyone, but they can all make it work, and I'm grateful. They don't know we're celebrating my amazing news from work today, just think it's a get-together before I leave on my work trip.

"Got it. We've got a table for six people at six forty-five," he says after tapping away at his phone's screen for a minute. I'm guessing, making the reservation, now that I know how many people we need it for. "Did Ellie not want to come?" he asks.

"No. I guess she's got a group project she's working on tonight with her best friend, so she's just eating over at her house."

"Ah, I hated those in school," he says.

"Me too."

"With dinner plans in place, come here," he says, curling his finger in a come-hither motion. My body is already tingling at the thought of the pleasure I know this man can bring to me.

"Do you remember back to my first road trip, after we started seeing one another?" he asks as I stop just a short distance from him.

"Yeah, why?" I ask, curious where this is going.

"Do you remember telling me about your fantasy?"

"Kind of. Why?"

"Because I'm going to make it a reality." He smirks before placing a kiss on the corner of my lips. "Clasp your hands, but leave one set of fingers up," he tells me, and it all comes rushing back.

I do as asked, and he slides one of his hands over mine, clasping mine with his. He pulls my hands up and over my head, backing me into the wall behind me, just like the couple in the video I watched did and I thought was so sexy and a turn-on.

"Am I doing this right?" he asks, looking down at me. I'm at his complete mercy and loving every second of it.

I nod my head in agreement, waiting for his next move.

"Good," he says before sliding a knee between my legs and dropping his lips to mine in a searing kiss. I press against his leg, the pressure giving me just a hint of relief where I need him most. "I like this, you at my mercy," Aiden says as his lips slide across my skin and down the column of my neck.

"Pure torture," I tell him. "I can hardly move," I say as I slide my head sideways, giving him easier access to my neck.

"Perfect. I can tease you, get you really riled up before I devour you." I feel him smirk against my skin.

"I'd complain, but what good would it do me?" I quip.

"More torture, but in a good way." He smiles at me and steps back. He lets go of me and lets my arms fall, which causes my hands to go tingly as the blood rushes down. I shake them out, hoping the feeling will go away quickly. "Did I hurt you?" he asks, concern lacing his voice.

"No, just going to sleep from the sudden movement of being over my head and then dropped after so long."

"I'm so sorry, babe," he says, rubbing at them, trying to help the blood circulate.

"It really isn't a big deal. No different than my foot going to sleep after sitting on it. I'll be fine in just a minute. If you're really upset about it, I can think of a few ways you could make it up to me," I purr, bringing his attention back to the sexy times I was hoping we were about to start.

"What do you have in mind?" he asks as he sweeps me up off my feet and carries me back to the bedroom.

"Maybe your tongue on my clit," I suggest.

"Yes, ma'am." He sets me at the end of the bed and starts to strip. I watch, then follow suit when he's almost completely naked. "About time you caught up." He strokes his already hard cock.

"Change of plans," I tell him as I drop to my knees. Aiden is very much a giver when it comes to oral. He'd happily go down on me without thinking I need to reciprocate. I don't complain because the man knows how to use his tongue on the clit. I grip his cock, stroking it a few times before bringing his tip to my lips. I place a few wet kisses on the tip, swirling my tongue around the sensitive head.

"Fucking fuck," he curses as he gathers my hair into a fist, holding it out of my way before I slide down his length. The head of his cock fills my throat, and I have to remind myself to breathe around it so I don't trigger my gag reflex. I hum with him in the back of my throat, knowing it drives him wild when I do. "Tori." He moans my name, which just eggs me on. I bob up and down his length, using my fist to encase the length I don't fit in my mouth. He starts to thrust lightly, and I stop my own motions so he can take control.

I'm not surprised when he slows his thrusts and pulls out of my mouth. "I need you on the bed, now," he says, pulling me up by the armpits.

I scurry up, lying back on the bed, opening my legs to accommodate him as he follows me into place. "These devilish lips," he growls as he kisses me. "They can make a man go weak in the knees." He kisses me again, this time thrusting inside me.

"Aiden," I cry out as I break our kiss. My body reacts to the sudden intrusion of his cock; he's already so close to his orgasm, he pounds into me, not starting out slowly like he'd normally do.

"Get there, Tori," he warns me. "I'm not going to last much longer this round."

I slide a hand between our bodies, thrumming my clit to aid my body along. My eyes fly open when he suddenly stops and pulls out. "Get on your hands and knees," he tells me as he helps to flip me over. As soon as I'm on all fours, he enters me from behind, holding on to my hips as he finds his punishing but oh-so-good rhythm again. I return to playing with my clit, as I can feel his cock swelling as his orgasm nears. His fingertips dig into my hips, and I'm sure they'll leave little love marks on my skin for the next few days. "Come with me," he whispers as he leans forward, his front covering my back as he places kisses along my shoulder. He slides a hand from my hip around to my clit, taking over the strumming of it until I'm flying over the edge and crying out his name. He comes right with me, calling my name as he falls over the cliff. We both collapse on the bed, his weight holding me to the mattress, but one I've come to love over the past few months. I know he's really spent and came hard when he doesn't immediately roll off of me. I've told him many times, he isn't hurting me when he pins me to the mattress, but he's always so worried he might.

As soon as he's gathered his strength, he rolls off, taking me with him. "Fuck, that was intense," he says as we curl up together. I can already feel his release leaking out as we forwent the condom. We tend to go in cycles of using them, ever since that one shower when I told him I was okay with him not wearing one.

"I need to go clean up. I think we're already too late and will have to change the sheets before bed tonight," I tell him as I push away so I can roll over and off the bed.

"God, you are sexy," he says as he watches me stand up and walk into the bathroom. I've learned to love my body even more than I did before since we've been together. After his one comment a while back that he wishes I could see myself through his eyes, I've tried really hard to not be so tough on myself. In the process of not being so harsh, I've actually lost a few pounds and toned up the areas that I always thought were my problem areas. Sometimes all it takes is a different outlook, and things magically click into place.

"You're the sexy one," I call out over my shoulder before I disappear into the bathroom.

I can hear him chuckling. This is an argument we

have often, trying to see who can be the last one to say it.

"I'm going to jump into the shower. I don't want to go to dinner smelling like sex," I tell him after I turn it on.

"Is that an invitation to join you?" he asks, a hopeful smile tugging at his lips.

"If you'd like, but no sexy times. I'm already sore, and I know we've got more to come after dinner," I tell him.

"I didn't hurt you, did I?" he asks, jumping out of bed and coming quickly to my side.

"Not in a bad way. I just don't want to be squirming at dinner and causing a scene. That first thrust was a little intrusive, so let's give the pussy a little bit of time to recuperate before you give it another good pounding. Sound good?" I ask, patting his chest.

"As long as I didn't hurt you, okay." He leans down and kisses me gently, as if he kisses me hard, I'll break.

"Thank you," I tell him. I step away and into the shower. The double showerheads in here are probably my favorite amenity of his condo, other than the view, that is.

CHAPTER 14
AIDEN

I escort Tori into the restaurant, my hand on the small of her back. We get a few turned heads as we walk in. I'd like to think it's because of the beautiful woman with me, but more than likely, it is because people recognize me. My face is splashed around the city on team advertising.

I approach the hostess stand and check in with the young woman behind it. "Is your entire party here?" she asks. I look around, but don't see the others. We are a few minutes early, so it doesn't surprise me.

"No, the others should be here shortly," I tell her.

"Would you like to wait for them before being seated, or we can show them back once they arrive," she offers.

"Being seated would be great," I tell her, flashing her what I like to call, my PR smile. It's the one I give all the reporters when they interview me.

"Right this way, Sir," she says after grabbing the large menus.

My hand goes right to Tori's back as we follow the hostess to our oval-shaped table, which is set for six. "Your server will be with you shortly," she mentions as she hands us menus, then places the others on top of the place settings.

"Thank you," Tori says before she walks away. I didn't miss how she ignored Tori, yet eye fucked me the entire time. That shit pisses me off, but I let it go since we're here to celebrate Tori's accomplishment, and I don't want anything to ruin our night.

"Hey, sorry we're late," Tori's mom gushes as they reach the table. I stand up, accepting her dad's outstretched hand in a firm shake.

"Good to see you again, Robert," I greet him before kissing Whitney on the cheek. "You look lovely tonight, Whitney. "

"You look pretty handsome yourself," she replies, patting me on the cheek. Tori is the spitting image of her mother.

"You aren't late at all. We only sat about a minute or two before you arrived, and we're still waiting for Ryker and Avery to get here," Tori tells her parents.

"Oh good. I didn't want to be the reason you were held up," Whitney states as she takes the seat next to Tori. Robert takes the one next to her, leaving two open seats between him and me for Avery and Ryker.

"We're here," Avery calls out as they approach the table.

"There was a backup at the valet stand," Ryker explains.

"Ah yes, we had the same issue," Robert adds as he

shakes Ryker's hand. Avery exchanges pleasantries with Tori's parents before we all settle in, then our server approaches to take our drink order.

We all order drinks from the bar. Tori and I are ready to celebrate with everyone at the table. The server returns only a couple of minutes later with everyone's drinks, which makes the perfect time to call a toast.

"I want to toast Tori tonight. She got some exciting news at work today, and I thought, what better way to celebrate than with the most important people in her life," I say to the silent table. Everyone lifts their glasses in a toast.

"What's your good news?" her mom asks.

"I met with George today. I mainly went in to ensure he didn't have any last-minute requests before I fly out tomorrow. He handed me a letter, my annual review. At the bottom of the review was a personalized paragraph from him. They more than doubled my salary, increased some of my other benefits, and told me I'm one of their best assets and wanted to ensure I knew. He said they'd like to know I'm willing to stay with them for the long run," she boasts, the excitement rolling off her as she tells everyone her good news.

"That's excellent, dear," Robert congratulates her.

"I'm so proud of you," Whitney adds.

"Congratulations," Avery and Ryker tell her as we all clink glasses once again.

"I'd say this was a much-earned celebration dinner," Robert adds. "Thanks for inviting us, kiddo."

"Thanks, Dad. I wouldn't dream of celebrating such

an accomplishment without the two of you," she tells him.

Our server returns, looking to take our order. We rattle off a few of the appetizers, giving us all time to still look over the main menu.

"Are you all ready for your trip tomorrow?" Whitney asks. Our appetizers start to arrive, and we all dig in.

"I think so. I packed most of my stuff over the weekend. I'm limiting myself to two suitcases since space on the bus is limited. If I really need something I didn't pack, I can always go buy it wherever we are."

"What time do you leave tomorrow?" Avery asks.

"I'm meeting my team at the airport at nine. With us taking the company plane, we don't have to be there super early. There isn't even really security. They'll walk us out onto the tarmac and right onto the plane. The flight attendant emailed me the other day, asking for our preference for food and drink."

"Sounds so fancy," Whitney comments.

"Bougie for sure," Avery adds.

"Just perks of the job." Tori shrugs.

"Look at our baby girl, a big wig boss, making her way in this world, flying private all over the place," Robert gushes to his wife. "How did we get so lucky to be blessed with such a wonderful daughter?"

"I don't know, but we got lucky, that's for sure," Whitney tells him.

"Stop, guys. You're going to make me cry," Tori says as she dabs at the corner of her eyes.

"No tears tonight." Whitney pats her hand. "Only if they're happy ones, I guess," she adds.

We enjoy our time with our friends and Tori's parents. We had dinner with them a month or so ago when she was finally ready to introduce them to me. Her dad had lots of questions about my profession and what my intentions were with his daughter. I expected it; she is their little girl, after all, even if she is in her late twenties. It was done in good faith because she's his only daughter. I get it. I'm sure I'll be the same way if we have a little girl and she brings a guy home for me to meet.

The server returns again, all our plates have been cleared from the table, and offers the dessert menu. "Anyone partaking?" I ask the table at large.

"I'm so full, so none for me," Tori states.

"Same. I can't eat one more bite, but thank you," Avery declines.

Everyone else follows suit, and I tell the server to bring the check to me.

"Are you sure? I don't mind chipping in," Ryker offers.

"Your money is no good to me." I wave him off. He backs off, knowing I won't accept his offer, even if he presses harder.

I sign the slip, adding in a nice tip since they took good care of us tonight.

"We hope you have a wonderful trip. Keep me updated on how everything goes," Whitney tells Tori as she pulls her in for a big hug. I take a moment to shake Robert's hand and thank him for coming out tonight.

"Of course. We'd never miss an invite from our girl. Maybe we can have the two of you out to the house once she's back, and it works with your game schedule."

"I'd like that, Sir, and I'm sure Tori would, as well. If you'd ever like to catch a game, we can get you set up with some free tickets."

"I might take you up on your offer. I haven't yet been to a live game, caught a few on TV these past few weeks, but still can't say I understand what's happening out there." Robert chuckles.

"I feel the same way sometimes," I joke.

We all say our goodbyes and head to our respective homes.

I HIT THE ICE, MY BODY A LITTLE SLUGGISH AFTER THE drinks from dinner last night, followed by a late bedtime and early wake-up. I had to send my girl off well-fucked and stocked up on orgasms.

"You going to make it through practice today?" Ryker asks, skating alongside me.

"I'm a bit tired, but a good ass kicking will do me some good." I smirk as I push off into a sprint around the rink.

"I'm sure you are," he says as he catches up. "Did you get any sleep last night? Or were you guys up all night celebrating?"

"We got a few hours, but not much," I admit.

"Well then, I hope Coach drills your ass and wakes you up." He chuckles

"Fucker," I mumble just as Coach hits the ice and blows his whistle. We all gather around in a semi-circle in front of him. His big whiteboard looks like a sheet of ice with the face-off circles and all the markings the ice has. He draws out some plays he wants us to run, and we get to work. The shrill of the whistle being blown every minute or so has my head pounding with a headache before the halfway mark of practice.

Once we're done with the first set of plays, I skate to the bench where our equipment and medical staff watch us from. "Can I get some Advil?" I ask, knowing they keep it on hand.

"Everything all right?" Teri, one of the trainers, asks.

"Yeah, just a killer headache. The whistle isn't helping much." I chuckle as he hands over a few pills. I knock them back, squirting some cold water into my mouth from the water bottle sitting on the edge of the boards.

"I'll get you a shake made up for when practice is over, help pump you full of some extra vitamins and electrolytes," he tells me.

"Thanks," I tell him before I skate back to my team-mates, who are running drills, now.

"If this is what it feels like when we're gone, I have a whole new respect for what you ladies go through," I say to Avery. Ryker invited me over for dinner tonight, and since I had nothing better to do, I took him up on the offer.

"Aw, are you missing our girl," Avery asks.

"Fuck yes, I am, and she's only been gone a day. How the hell am I going to last three weeks without seeing her?"

"You'll get used to it, I promise. Just try not to look at the clock or your phone all the time. And for the love of God and all that is holy, do not blow up her phone if you don't hear back from her immediately. She's in a different time zone, will be working crazy hours, and will most likely be dead-ass tired when she isn't working."

"Did she tell you to say that to me?" I ask, worried I've pissed her off with the few texts I've sent her today.

"No, but should she have?" Avery chuckles.

"I haven't blown her phone up, much," I grumble. "I've only sent four texts since she left this morning," I tell her.

Avery and Ryker laugh at my expense, and I just let them. "You're an asshole." I point at Ryker but can't hold back from joining them. I feel like someone stole my puppy or some shit like that.

It does me some good to hang out with my friends. I find I've quit obsessing over not hearing back from Tori for a few more hours.

"All right, I should head home. I need a full night's sleep," I say as I stand and stretch.

"Thanks for coming over. I hope we got your mind off of missing your girl," Avery says sweetly.

"Thanks for putting up with my broody ass," I tell

her, giving her a side hug. I slap Ryker on the shoulder before heading for the exit.

"See you at practice tomorrow," he calls out as he follows me to the door.

"See you then. Hopefully, I won't be so sluggish tomorrow."

"I'll make sure to kick your ass in the weight room if you are." He smirks before closing the door behind me.

I head home, missing Tori horribly. I seriously don't know how I'm going to make it the next few weeks without her here. I've never missed her like this when I'm on the road, so I don't know why it is affecting me so badly now that she's the one gone and I'm at home.

I drive home in silence. I turned off the radio after pulling out onto the highway, as the music just reminded me of her. I pull into the garage and am just about to kill the engine when the shrill of my phone ringing over the Bluetooth fills the space.

"Hello," I answer, hoping like hell it is Tori.

"Hey." Her sweet but very tired voice fills my ears.

"Hey, baby. How are you? How was your day?" I ask, and grab my cell from the cup holder. I move the call over to my phone and kill the car engine.

"Busy, long, and oh so tiring," she says, and I can hear her yawning. "How was yours?"

"Are you sleeping on the bus tonight or in a hotel?" I ask. There was some uncertainty this morning before she left about the bus being ready for them tonight. Something about a delay in a part coming in to fix whatever broke on its last assignment.

"We're in a hotel for tonight and tomorrow night. It

works out, since we aren't leaving here for a few more days as it is."

"That's good. My day was pretty meh. I was sluggish at practice and got a splitting headache about halfway through. I had to stop and get some painkillers. I went over to Ryker and Avery's for dinner for a few hours. I think they both took pity on me, knowing I would be in a shit mood with you gone. She read me the riot act about not bombarding you with calls and texts." I chuckle as I remember her giving me the mom voice.

"Sounds like my best friend, but just know, if she was willing to do that to you, it means she likes you and thinks you're good for me," Tori says.

"If you say so," I tell her as I make my way up the elevator and to my unit.

"Where are you?" she asks.

"I just walked in the door from having dinner and bullshitting with them."

"Oh, yeah, it's three hours earlier there than it is here." She laughs at her own mix-up. "God, I'm exhausted. I don't know how you deal with all the travel."

"You get used to it. What kind of hours do you think you'll be pulling tomorrow?"

"Probably a sixteen-hour day." She groans. "We've got semi-trailers of merchandise to log into the system, along with supervising the setup of the fan experience zone. With this being our first stop, we're taking a few extra days to make sure we know exactly how to get it all done. In most cities, the crew will only have a half a day to get it all done, so they're setting it up and tearing it down multiple times here."

"Sounds exhausting," I admit.

"Very, but they did a great job today, and I'm sure tomorrow will just get faster and more efficient."

"How much merchandise do you have left to log?"

"We're down to one last trailer to sort and log in. More is on order and will be shipped to whatever cities it's needed in. They ordered what they hope is enough to last the first half of the tour. We'll watch inventory counts as items sell, which will also give us a better idea of what fans are actually wanting and what ended up not being popular this tour," she explains.

"Is the band there already?"

"Yeah, they arrived today, as well. They wanted a couple days to practice on their travel stage. They've been practicing in a warehouse the past couple of weeks, but being on the actual stage makes a difference. It will also give the sound people a chance to tweak things, not that they won't still have to do sound checks at each venue, as the sound can change based on the venue quite a bit."

"Are they nice?"

"Yes, so nice. Their tour manager is kind of an asshole at times, but it's also part of his job." She chuckles. "It's his job to keep them on schedule and weed out all the nonsense that comes with being a sought-after band, but he can sometimes be an asshole simultaneously."

"I hope for your sanity he's on his best behavior while you're on tour."

"Eh, thankfully, we don't need his approval for anything we're doing, so unless I need direct access to the band, we don't really have to cross paths."

"That's good. You don't need any more stress than you already have."

"That's for damn sure. I was so excited for this trip, and I'm sure it will get better as the days go by, but damn, I wasn't expecting it to be this tiring. I also misjudged how long our days were going to be."

"Be kind to yourself. You did just travel across the country on little sleep, then hit the ground running. Anyone would be exhausted in your shoes."

"Thanks." She yawns again.

"Babe, why don't you go get ready for bed and call it a night? We can talk again tomorrow."

"Yeah, I probably should," she agrees. "I just don't know if I have the energy to actually get up and put my PJs on, I might just sleep in the clothes I have on."

"You know you'll regret it in the morning. A few more minutes tonight will allow you to sleep so much better."

"Why do you have to be so right?" She snickers.

"Because I've been exactly where you are and did sleep in my suit and really regretted it come morning," I state.

"Ugh, fine, I'm getting up now."

"Love you, sleep tight and call or text me tomorrow."

"Love you, too. I have no idea what time it will be, but I will."

"Your team is going to kick ass, just remember that."

"Thanks for your confidence. I think we need it after today."

"Night, sweetheart," I tell her before she disconnects the call.

Now that I've finally talked to her today, my nerves aren't so shot. I know she's doing what she loves and will kill it. I just hate this soul-deep feeling of missing her.

CHAPTER 15
TORI

THE PAST TEN DAYS HAVE BEEN SO MUCH FUN. THE TOUR started, and the feedback from fans has blown us out of the water. They love the new fan experience we are offering, along with the merchandise outside the venue. It has helped tremendously with the crowds inside, so we plan to implement this setup with all tours going forward.

With the long days and not the greatest sleeping conditions, I've become really run down and feel like I'm getting sick. We've only got four more days before we return home, so I'm hopeful I'll make it back without anything serious being wrong. It might take a week straight of sleeping to feel human again, but I'll make it. I swear, this is worse than the six weeks I spent in Africa last year.

"Hey, Tori, are you in here?" Quinn calls from the doorway to the bus.

I'm sitting in the rear of the bus where the mobile office is set up. "Yeah, I'm back here," I call out. He comes back, a laptop in his hands, as he takes a seat across from me. "What's up?" I ask.

"I was just going over inventory, and we're going through two items twice as fast as we predicted. If the trend continues, we'll run out in about five more shows. Do you want me to go ahead and have the order fulfilled to restock those items and have them sent to the venue they'll be at in, say, four shows?"

"Sounds reasonable to me. What two items is it?"

"This sweatshirt," he says, and turns his screen so I can see it. "And this T-shirt," he says, and turns it again for me.

"Ah, yeah, I noticed both of those being super popular when I've been in the merchandise booth. Are we noticing a trend on all sizes, or do we need more of some and not others?"

"It's been pretty consistent. I think placing a reorder of all sizes would be the best option," he tells me as he types away at his computer. "Plus, we get the best price that way, and it keeps the profit margins the best."

"You've done your homework," I praise him. "Forward the order request, and I'll get it approved."

"Thanks, Tori," he says. "Are you feeling any better this morning?"

"I think so. I ate some toast and oatmeal and drank a cup of coffee. I think it is just all the long days catching up with me. I'm definitely ready for my bed back," I tell him.

"I can't agree more with you on that one. I don't know how these bands do this road life for months and months. I'm ready to be done after a week and a half."

"They say you get used to it. I'm sure their beds are a little nicer than ours are, since this is a short-use bus."

"I'd sure hope so. I also hope their bunks are longer." He chuckles. The poor guy is almost taller than the bunks are long in here.

"Yeah, it would definitely be a must for long-term. I hate you are so cramped in the bunk." I grimace.

"Not your fault, and I'll survive. I'm used to being crammed in small places. Comes with being tall my entire life."

"If we do this again, I'll make sure to ask if they have any buses with extra-long bunks," I promise him.

"Deal." He smiles at me. "Alright, I should get back to work. Holler if you need anything," he offers before unfolding himself from the chair and heading back out.

I pull up the email he sent showing the order we just discussed. I verify all the numbers and send it to production. They'll start on it as soon as possible, so they make sure it is delivered to whatever city the band will be in on the date specified in the order. It's amazing how many moving parts must come together to keep a multi-billion dollar-tour running smoothly. From catering to merchandise, there is always something being tweaked daily.

I make a good dent in my emails and the computer work I needed to get caught up on. Just because I'm on tour right now doesn't mean my daily tasks can go by the wayside. I'm also excited to meet with Reese Blackwood after I return. Nothing has been set in stone yet for her next tour, but it sounds like that will be happening in the coming months. I know she's been working on some new music, which I can't wait to hear, so we have a lot to work on once I get back.

My stomach growls. I flick my eyes to the clock and see it is already two o'clock. I've completely missed lunchtime, but I'm starving, so I head in search of the catering room. Because the crew works almost non-stop from the time we arrive at a new venue until show time, the catering department keeps food on hand the entire day.

I add a half sandwich to my plate and a handful of chips, then grab a bowl of soup and go find a place to sit outside in the sun. We're in Florida today, and the sun feels warm on my skin.

I'm scrolling through TikTok when my phone rings. Aiden's face pops up, and I can't help but get giddy our time apart is almost over.

"Hey, babe," I greet as I place my phone to my cheek.

"Hey, how's your day?" he asks.

"Eh, started off kind of meh. I was feeling run down this morning, but I'm feeling better now. Had a light breakfast and am just now having lunch. How's your day?"

"Mine's fine. On my way home after our morning skate. I didn't skate but went in to have some work done on my hip and legs. I was feeling super tight after the last game and the hit I took."

"How'd it go?" I ask. I missed the game, but he told me all about the hit. I Googled until I found a clip of it, and it didn't look good. He left the ice shortly after it and stayed off for the rest of the period.

"It hurt like a bitch, but I think it's getting better. Just some muscle tightness and bruising. Nothing was seriously damaged."

"That's good but take it easy. Sit this one out if you need to. It would be better to miss one game as a precaution than to injure yourself badly and be out for weeks or months."

"I'll see how it's feeling after my nap, and talk to the trainers and coach, and make it a game-time decision."

"Sounds like a solid plan."

"I can't wait to see you next week," Aiden says.

"I know. It's torture knowing you won't be home when I get back," I tell him.

"You could always fly to Chicago instead of San Francisco. Come stay with me at the hotel," he says.

I muse over his suggestion. "I'll think about it and let you know, how does that sound?"

"I'll do whatever it takes to get you there. I miss you so fucking much."

"Okay, caveman," I tease him, but love he misses me just as much as I miss him. Also, knowing he wants me to fly to his away game just hits differently.

"I'm serious, Tori. Figure out a way to get yourself to Chicago. Hell, I'll book your ticket myself if you want, but I need you. I need to kiss those sweet lips. I need to eat your even sweeter pussy, and I need to slide so deep inside you we can't tell where I end and you begin."

I'm sure my cheeks are flaming red right now from his words. My center is already throbbing, and there's not much I can do to take care of the feeling, seeing as how I'm sharing a tour bus with four other people. Not much privacy available outside of the not-so-big bathroom.

"Are you still there?" Aiden asks.

"Yeah, you just left me a little speechless."

"What can I say? I just miss you so fucking bad. It's like I've lost a damn limb, and if I can see you a few days early, then dammit, I'm going to make it happen."

"I'll check things tonight," I promise him.

"Sounds good, babe. Text me your flight info when you have it booked."

"Hold your horses." I laugh. "Don't you need to go take your nap?" I ask him, trying to turn the conversation off of me coming to him.

"I need to eat lunch, first, and then I'll lie down."

"Then go eat and take a nap. I hope you feel good enough to play tonight, but don't push it. I don't want you seriously hurt."

"But if I get hurt, then you can be my sexy bedside nurse," he says, and I can just imagine the smirk on his face. "I like that idea, you in a sexy nurse outfit, maybe with no panties so I can slip two fingers inside you while you're standing bedside and make you cum. Maybe flip the skirt up and have you sit right down on my lap, sliding my hard length inside you. Fuck, baby, I'm hard just imagining all the naughty things I could do to you while I'm laid up and recovering."

"You have such a dirty, *dirty*, mind," I tell him. "Please don't ever change."

"Fuckin vixen," he mumbles. "I guess I'll be taking a

shower before my nap and thinking of your sweet pussy as I come in my hand."

"You're welcome," I sing-song. "You always play with an extra pep after a game day quickie."

"Damn straight, I do. Even more the reason for you to meet me on the road trip. Think of how much better I'll play after I fuck you, plus, we'll be in a hotel. Isn't there something to be said about hotel sex?"

"Some people like to say hotel sex is better because it's a random location. I can't confirm nor deny if it's true or not," I tell him.

"Then let's find out," he quips.

"We'll see," I tell him again. "I'm being flagged down. I need to go. I'll talk to you later, okay?"

"Okay, love you. Glad you're feeling better."

"Thanks, me too. Love you," I tell him before I end the call. I grab my trash, toss it in the can, and then jog over to where Cassandra and Rebecca are standing and waiting for me.

THE PORTION OF THE TOUR WE'RE FOLLOWING HAS JUST come to an end. I collapse in one of the chairs in one of the back rooms of the arena, my body exhausted from the last two weeks. We pulled it off and didn't have any significant setbacks to deal with.

"To a successful trip," Quinn calls out in a toast to the group.

"Here, here," the others call out.

"I'm so proud of the work we accomplished," I tell

all of them. "You all really stepped up and kicked ass. Be ready for a new project when we return to the office next week. I was given word before I left that Reese Blackwood will be flying into town to meet with us. She wants to be hands-on with developing all the PR going into her new album release and subsequent tour, so start brainstorming now for any cool new ideas you might have we can suggest."

"Awesome!" Rebecca cheers. "I love her so much."

"She's one of my favorite artists to work with, so this should be fun. I also can't wait to hear her new music. I haven't gotten any news about it, so I'm not even sure what this record's vibe will be like."

"Maybe we should wait to make too many suggestions until after we know?" Will suggests.

"Oh, absolutely. I know we want to include the fan experience. It has been such a success with this tour, and I know Reese will love the idea."

"Done," Quinn says.

"Did you ever decide if you were going to fly back to San Francisco with us in the morning or to Chicago to meet up with Aiden?" Rebecca asks.

"I found a ticket to Chicago. I just haven't told him yet." I smile at them. "I wanted to surprise him. I'm just trying to figure out how, exactly, I'm going to do so. The hotel won't give me a key to his room without his approval, so I can't just be waiting in his room when he gets back."

"Can one of the other guys help you out?" Cassandra asks.

"Maybe." I mull over the idea. "I could text Ryker

and see what he suggests. My other idea is to just hang out in the lobby until he walks in and then follow him to the elevator. Maybe pretend I'm some fan who really wants to rock his world up in his room and see what his reaction is." I smirk.

"I like that one," Rebecca says. "But only if you record it so we can see his reaction."

"It might not end up being work appropriate," I joke, but knowing Aiden, he'll be ready to strip me the moment he sees me.

"Well, whatever you do, have a good time." Cassandra winks at me.

"I plan on it," I say. "All right, let's get out of here and back to the bus so we can all pack up. I have a shuttle scheduled to pick you guys up at nine to take you to the airport. I'll be taking a separate shuttle simultaneously, but over to the main airport."

"Thanks for getting it all set up," Quinn says.

"Of course. Once I got the flight info for your return back to San Francisco, I made it a priority. Enjoy your next few days off, and I'll see you all in the office next week."

We all head back to the bus and get busy packing up everything before we all crash. Everyone is a zombie when the alarms start ringing a few hours later, but we all make it off the bus and on our way to the airports on time.

CHAPTER 16
AIDEN

I skate around the rink, a little pissed Tori wasn't able to make it work to fly here to Chicago and then on to Vegas with me for this short road trip. I understand she's the boss and had some meetings to get back for, but fuck, I miss her.

"You ready to hit the showers?" Ryker asks as he skates up alongside me.

"I guess," I tell him as I push my helmet back and wipe a hand over my face.

"Are you still salty because Tori's not coming in today?"

"Hell yes, I'm salty. Fucking meeting," I grumble, and he just laughs.

"Do I need to take you out and get you drunk tonight after the game to make it better?"

"No, I'll get over it."

"Yeah, when we get back to California," he muses. "It could be worse. She could be gone weeks, if not months, longer."

"Fuck that."

"A little double standard, there. You can travel for work and expect her to not have any issues with it, but when she has to, you throw a hissy fit like a toddler?"

"Hell, when you put it like that, I feel like an asshole. I guess I better go call her and apologize."

"Probably isn't a bad idea. I hear women like diamonds, flowers, and trips to exotic places," he tells me.

Ryker mentioning diamonds has an image of me down on one knee, holding up a diamond ring to Tori, asking her to be mine forever. While I know deep down we haven't been together long enough for me to ask her, we're definitely headed in that direction. I don't think it would make her run in the other way, at this point, as I think we're both at the same place in our relationship,

"I'll think of something," I assure him as we both leave the ice and head for the locker room.

I take a quick shower, changing back into the street clothes I wore to practice. I don't have to don a suit until we leave the hotel for the game later.

I hop onto the bus and pull out my phone to see if I've missed any messages from Tori letting me know she's made it back. Checking the time, I see it isn't late enough yet for them to have made it back, since they weren't flying out until around ten. She should arrive while I'm napping, so I'll talk to her for a little bit after I wake up.

The bus finally leaves the rink and makes the twenty-minute drive to the hotel. When we pull up, a small crowd stands outside, hoping to get pictures and signatures from the players. I'm in a shitty enough of a mood I just press on and head straight into the hotel and up to my room.

I open my door and walk in, ready to order some room service and collapse into bed. However, my eyes about pop out of my head when I see the most beautiful image. Tori is curled up on my bed and fast asleep. How in the hell did she get in here, I wonder.

"Tori, baby." I walk over to the edge of the bed, rubbing her shoulder lightly to wake her up. Her eyes pop open, and she gives me a sleepy smile.

"Surprise, I'm here," she says, yawning as she sits up.

"When did you get in? How did you get into my room? I have so many questions, but fuck them, kiss me now," I say as I hover over her on the bed. "I've missed the fuck out of you," I say as I drop my lips to hers in the most anticipated kiss of my life so far.

I don't let her up from underneath me for a good solid twenty minutes, getting my fill of our mouths connecting.

"I need you inside me," Tori says after we break apart.

"My pleasure," I tell her as I stand to strip. She quickly follows suit, and moments later, I'm hovering over top of her once again, this time sliding my cock into her pussy. The way her walls instantly grip my cock has me seeing stars. I slowly pull out, just to push right back in. I keep my strokes slow and sensual. I don't want to rush this, much to my balls' disappointment, and need to release.

"I've missed you so much," Tori says as she runs her hands through my hair. I kiss the tip of her nose, then her cheeks, as I continue the slow and torturous rhythm.

"Same, baby, so damn much. I realize I was being unfair to you. And I'm sorry if I was an asshole about the time apart. You've never complained about the travel required with my job; I shouldn't complain about yours."

"It's okay, I forgive you," she says as her body clenches around mine. "Harder, Aiden," she tells me.

I can't deny her anything, so I pick up the pace, giving her what she's asked for. "Fuck, baby, I'm going to come."

"Me too," she says as our eyes connect once again.

The air crackles around us as we both fall over the edge. I can't imagine my life with anyone else. She's it for me. I just have to be patient, so I can make it my reality.

CHAPTER 17
TORI

I hate I fell asleep while I waited for Aiden to return to the hotel, but I was so damn tired. Even with falling asleep, my surprise still was a good one.

I finally confessed to him that Avery and I came up with the plan. We both flew in, and she got a key from Ryker, who apparently slipped the second one out of Aiden's pocket when he was on the ice and Ryker was in the locker room yesterday. Ryker gave it to Avery to give to me when she picked me up from the airport.

Avery and I meet up once the guys are gone. They have to leave for the rink hours early. Much earlier than we are allowed into the rink as spectators. Ryker also took care of getting the two of us some tickets to the game, that way, we could be in the building cheering our men on.

"How'd the surprise go?" Avery asks as we walk down the street to the nearest Starbucks.

"I fell asleep, but other than that, he was definitely shocked," I tell her.

"I wish I could have seen the look on his face when he saw you," she says.

"Me too. I'm sure it was priceless. The face I got when he woke me up was so sweet," I tell her.

"Did he ever get a nap?" She smirks.

"Eventually, but we had some catching up to do," I tell her.

"I'm sure you did." She tosses her head back with a laugh.

We step up to the counter, and both place our orders. I'm in some desperate need of caffeine if I'm going to make it through the game tonight. I'm already dragging ass.

"Where is Ellie staying while you're gone?" I ask once we have our drinks and find a table to sit at.

"Her best friend's house. She was so excited I could make this trip work, so I took it as a good sign."

"I'm glad you were able to join me. Plus, I needed your help to pull off my surprise."

"I'm sure you'd have been able to pull something off had I not been able to make it," she says.

"Maybe," I tell her, as my stomach rolls. I set my cup down and cover my mouth with a hand.

"Is everything okay? You look like you might puke," she says, concern lacing her voice.

"I've been so run down the last week. I think the long days, crappy sleep, and not the healthiest food is catching up to me," I tell her. "I will get these random feelings of nausea, but they go as fast as they come. I haven't puked, but man, do they hit me so randomly."

"How long has this been happening?" she asks.

"Maybe the last week?" I tell her, thinking back to when it started.

"Is that when the exhaustion started?" she asks.

I try to think back, and I can't remember for sure, as I swear I was exhausted from the first day.

"I don't think so, but it's hard to know since I was pulling such long days the entire time. Why, what are you thinking?"

"Could you be pregnant?" she asks.

The thought never even crossed my mind, since I'm on the pill.

"I don't think so. We usually use condoms, and I'm on the pill. You know how I am with taking it at the same time every day."

"Is your period late?" she asks, and I whip out my phone to check my period tracker app. My face must go ghostly white when I look at the screen and see that I should have started two days ago. "How late are you?" she asks.

"Just two days, but my cycle is always like clock-work." I start to sweat. My stomach rolls again as my nerves start to go crazy. What will Aiden think if I'm pregnant? Would he think I was trying to trap him? Would he be excited about a baby? So many unknowns.

"Take a deep breath. We can walk over to the drugstore and pick up a test. Do you want to take it before the game or wait until Aiden is with you?" Avery sweetly asks.

"I don't know. What do you think?" I ask her. I need my best friend now more than ever.

"Well, do you want to be able to tell him you already know the answer, or do you want to find out together?"

"I don't know. What do you think he'll say?" I ask her.

"Have the two of you ever talked about kids?" she asks, sympathy evident in her questions.

"Not specifically. We've both expressed the want to have a family down the road, but nothing specific, like, how many or when is the right time to settle down."

"I don't really think there is a perfect time. Sometimes you just have to go with what fate gives you and figure it out from there. Look at Ryker. He was just starting out in his career when Ellie was born. It wasn't ideal, but she happened, and he's made the best of it. If you asked him now, he wouldn't change the circumstances for anything, as that would mean he wouldn't have Ellie."

"I know you're right, but it is still scary as shit that this might be happening before it was truly planned. I thought we were covering our bases."

"Then, maybe if you are pregnant, this baby is just meant to be." She smiles at me. "There's a pharmacy just two blocks away. How about we head there and then go back to the hotel. You can either take one then, or wait until after the game and Aiden is back."

"Okay," I agree. I suddenly no longer want to drink it, so I toss my barely touched coffee into the trash.

We walk down the street, finding the pharmacy easily. Avery leads the way, directly to the aisle with all the pregnancy test options. I've never had to take one in my life, so I'm a little overwhelmed by the selection.

Some have pink lines, others have blue ones, and then there are the digital screens. Some claim to be sensitive enough to tell you five days before a missed period. Seeing as how I'm already late, that isn't an issue for me. I grab two boxes of the digital ones. Figure they'd be the easiest to read when the time comes.

I take my items to the register, handing over my credit card to the older man behind the counter, who rings me up.

Avery and I walk back to the hotel, making very little conversation. I'm still just so shocked I didn't realize I was late, nor did I put anything together and think they were pregnancy symptoms.

"Have you decided what you want to do?" Avery asks once we are back in Aiden's room.

"I think I'm going to wait. That way, we find out together."

"Solid plan. Do you still want to go to the game?" she asks.

"Yeah, I'd like to try. I think he'd freak out if I wasn't there."

"You're probably right," she agrees. "Can I get you anything before it's time to go? Do you just want to hang out or nap?"

"A nap sounds good, but it's already four thirty. I don't really have time for one."

"We can just veg here until around six, then walk over to the arena, if that works for you."

"Perfect. Are you okay with grabbing food there?" I ask. We'd discussed going out somewhere near the arena before we flew in, but I'm not sure I'm up for it right now.

"Perfectly fine with it. What about you? Are you going to be able to find anything at the rink that doesn't make you want to puke?"

"I should be fine. I haven't puked anything up yet, and we don't even know if I'm actually pregnant. It might all just be my body's way of dealing with the stress of being gone and the constant long days with little sleep."

"Maybe, but I think you should test to know for sure."

"I will, I promise," I tell her as we both kick back and relax until it is time to walk over to the rink.

Ryker got us family passes, so we can access the visitor side of the boards, which is limited to people with special access. Aiden comes over to the area where we're standing and opens the door. He pokes his head around the glass and gives me a sweet kiss. "Glad you made it," he says before stepping back and closing the door.

"Aw, that was so sweet," Avery coos beside me.

"Who knew they could secretly be such sweet men?"

"Oh, I've known. I always get a good chuckle at the images they have of Ryker looking all bad-ass, yet off the ice, he's nothing like you'd think he was by just looking at the image they use on all the adver-tisements."

"I've thought the same thing when I've seen his

broody face plastered around town. Like, how is that the same guy who's swept my best friend off her feet?"

Ryker skates by, tapping the end of his stick against the glass in front of us, and laughs when we both startle.

Avery glares at him, which makes him laugh even harder. "Pay attention, babe," he calls out to her.

"You're going to pay for that," she tells him.

"I'm not even going to ask what his punishment will be." I smirk.

"Oh, I'll think of something good and dirty."

"That's a girl. Make him work for it."

"Damn straight. I've never been with a man who's so attentive, if you know what I mean."

"Oh, I know. It must be something with the stamina or from being a professional athlete."

"Must be," she agrees as the warmups slow down and the time runs out. They clear the ice, and the rink's ice crew comes out to pick up all the pucks so the Zamboni can mop the ice and get it ready for the first period.

◆

"You played so well," I tell Aiden as he comes up to me after his game. He's still dressed in his gear, as he just left the ice. Our passes gave us access to the hallway the locker room is off of, so Avery and I headed down here with a few minutes left in the game so we could see the guys before heading back to the hotel. They'll be at least an hour behind us. They're staying the night here and flying to Vegas tomorrow. Usually, they leave right after the game, but I guess teams prefer to be in Vegas as little as possible to decrease the amount of free time the players have in the city where they can get into some trouble, if they aren't careful.

"Thanks, it was the extra pep in my game that did it." He winks, referencing the pre-game sex we had.

"I'm sure it was." I push up and kiss him.

"Are you waiting around or heading back?" he asks.

"We're going to walk back, so I'll just see you when you get there."

"Okay, just be safe."

"Always," I tell him. I've felt pretty good since we came over for the game, not having any other episodes of nausea. I'm starting to second-guess the whole pregnancy thing, but I will talk to Aiden about it once we're alone, and we can decide if I should test and get it out of the way, together.

Avery and I make our way out of the building and follow the large crowd as they disperse to all the parking garages, hotels, and surrounding public transportation options.

We make it back to the hotel ten minutes later, and decide to grab a table in the hotel's bar and wait for the guys here. They have interviews, then will shower and load on the bus to be driven back over. They still take a bus even though they are just a few blocks away, for their safety.

"I texted Ryker to let him know where we are," Avery tells me once we're seated. I stuck with a Sprite, just in case.

"Perfect, I could see Aiden getting tunnel vision and heading straight up to the room, thinking that is where I'd be, and completely missing me." I laugh.

"Right? I think Ryker would do the same thing sometimes. I swear, they get one-track minds."

"Oh, don't even get me started," I tell her.

We chat it up until the guys arrive. They each grab a drink and join us at the table.

"Hey," Aiden says as he sits next to me, leaning over and placing a kiss on my cheek. "Having a good time?"

"Yes, although I'll be ready to go upstairs soon," I tell him as my stomach flops again. This time, I'm sure it is because of nerves and not from nausea.

"Whenever you're ready, we can go," he says. "Is everything okay?"

"Yeah," I tell him, and hope he can't see right through me.

We stick it out long enough for Aiden to drink his beer, then call it a night. Ryker and Avery are just as ready to head upstairs, so we all clear out simultaneously.

"Call me in the morning, once you're up. I think we have to leave for the airport around ten thirty," Avery says on our way up the elevator.

"Will do," I tell her, knowing she will want to know what happened tonight.

"Night," Ryker calls out as they step into his room. Aiden and I continue down the hall a little ways, until we reach his. It feels like it takes forever for the lock to click open and for us to step inside.

"What's wrong?" he asks as soon as the door is

closed. He pulls me into his arms, tilting my head up to look at him. It shouldn't surprise me that this man can sense when I'm in turmoil.

I blow out a big breath, ready to lay it all out for him, and so I do. I tell him about the symptoms and how Avery asked if I could be pregnant. How it made me look at my app. I told him about the tests in my bag but that I didn't test because I wanted him to be there if I tested, so we could find out together.

"Do you need to pee?" he asks, a smile already tugging at his lips.

"Yes," I answer. "Are you happy about this?" I ask, a little shocked.

"Hell yes, I am." He kisses me gently. "I plan to one day make you my wife. I want to fill a house with kids, so if you're pregnant now, I guess we're getting a head start. I just have to hope your dad doesn't shoot me for knocking you up before putting a ring on it," he tells me, and I just stand there, dumbfounded. I thought he'd be pissed.

"Is that not what you expected me to say?" he finally asks.

"No, no, it isn't," I tell him honestly. "I thought you'd be mad or upset, not excited."

"It isn't like you were poking holes in my condoms. I'm a big boy. I know birth control doesn't always work, and it was my decision just as much as it was yours to forgo condoms sometimes. If anything, I'm impressed with my sperm. It must be pretty potent if it can bypass your birth control."

"Of course, you'd think that." I chuckle.

"Now, get in there and pee in the damn cup, so I know if I need to work overtime to knock you up or if I've already done it."

"That's not how this works," I scold him.

He just laughs and follows me into the bathroom. I grab one plastic cup from the counter, unwrap it, and then sit down and pee into it. I set it on the counter and wash my hands before tearing into the first package. I don't really know why I bought two packages, since they both contain two tests, but it seemed logical, at the time.

"Can you hurry up, woman?" Aiden asks impatiently.

I read the instructions carefully, remove the cap and hold it in the liquid for a count of ten, then remove it and replace the lid. It's then I notice Aiden has opened his camera app and is recording all of this. He's propped the phone up on the bathroom counter as we wait the three minutes the instructions say we have to wait for the results.

I glance down at the timer on my phone, then to the test screen. It is still flashing a black line. The timer shows only thirty seconds have passed.

My heartbeat whooshes in my ears. My hands get all sweaty as my nerves go haywire.

"Just take a deep breath," Aiden tells me, turning me so I'm facing him. My back is to the counter, so I can no longer obsessively watch the timer and test. I follow his instruction and suck in a deep breath through my nose and blow it out of my mouth.

"Good, now again," he says, and does it with me.

"Perfect," he says before kissing me gently. "Whatever the test says, we'll face it together."

"Okay," I say as tears prick my eyes.

"I love you, Tori. A baby might not have been on our radar right now, but if we're blessed with one, we'll figure out how to be parents together."

"I can't imagine doing this with anyone else," I tell him honestly. He's calmed me down so much in just the last few minutes. I know deep down he's going to be a great dad and, hopefully one day, my husband.

CHAPTER 18
AIDEN

"Are you ready?" I ask Tori. The timer on her phone has gone off. I can't see the test because of how she's standing, but I just have a feeling it's going to be positive.

"As I'll ever be." She smiles up at me. I kiss her deeply one last time before she turns in my arms and grabs the test. The way she picks it up, her palm covers the screen, so we still don't know. "One, two, three," she counts out, and then moves her hand.

Positive

"Hell yes!" I call out as she turns back around, and I pick her up, twirling us around in a circle as we celebrate the news together.

"I-I'm speechless," she says as our lips connect.

"Super sperm," I tell her again. I remember I'm recording this, so I grab my phone and stop the video. We don't need any more video evidence of our celebrating. It isn't anything suitable for other eyes.

Four weeks later

"Victoria," the nurse calls out. Tori pops out of the chair, and I follow behind her as we make our way over to where the nurse stands at the open door. "Right this way," she says. "Can you confirm your last name and date of birth, please."

Tori rattles off both as we make our way to a little nook with a blood pressure machine, scale, and a few other medical gadgets.

"I just need to get your weight, a blood pressure, and then I'll have you leave a urine sample in the bathroom before you head into the exam room. Dad, if you want to come with me, I'll show you into the room now."

I follow her down the hall and step into a room with two waiting chairs, an exam table, a stool for the doctor, and a small counter with a sink. I've never been to an OBGYN office, so the posters on the wall are not ones I've seen before. All are pointing out different things to go with female anatomy.

I take a seat in one of the chairs and am joined by Tori a minute later.

"Go ahead and undress completely, placing this gown on and this blanket over your lap. We do a full exam during your first prenatal visit. The doctor might also send you for a dating ultrasound at the end. It's routine, so don't worry if she does send you for one."

"Thank you," Tori tells her.

The nurse leaves the room, and she strips down. I've noticed little changes in her body in the past few weeks. Her breasts are larger and super sensitive. I made her orgasm the other morning just by sucking on her nipples. It was the sexiest thing ever. I can't wait to see all the changes her body makes over the coming months.

"Tori," the middle-aged doctor greets as she enters the room.

"Dr. Morgan, it's nice to see you," Tori greets back.

"You must be the lucky dad." Dr. Morgan turns to me, offering her hand.

"Aiden, nice to meet you," I reply.

"Let's get the exam out of the way, and then I can answer any of your burning questions. I see we have your last menstrual cycle date. Did you still want a dating ultrasound?" she asks as she starts to check Tori out.

"If it's an option, I'd love to get a look at our baby," Tori tells her.

"Not a problem, at all. By my calculations, you're eight weeks along. We'll confirm with the ultrasound and give you a specific due date. How have you been feeling?"

"Tired, so very tired. I was nauseous in the early weeks but never puked, so I'm calling it a win."

"That's great," Dr. Morgan says. She moves up and presses around Tori's breasts. "Everything looks good to me. Do you have any questions?"

"It's okay for us to continue having sex, correct?" I ask as soon as she opens the floor for questions.

Tori rolls her eyes at me, but I need to know. I'd forgo if it were going to hurt the baby or her, but fuck if that's not a long time to go without her coming on my cock.

Dr. Morgan chuckles. "It's always the dad's first question," she tells Tori. "Sex is safe during pregnancy as long as there aren't any known complications. If Tori were put on pelvic rest or bed rest, then we'd take sex off the safe list, but as of now, it's a safe activity. Listen to your body. If something doesn't feel good, change positions. As the baby grows and the uterus stretches, some positions will no longer work. There are lots of other positions that will work and feel much better for both of you. As we get closer to the due date, sex can help kickstart labor, so don't be shocked if she's asking for it a lot at that point. The first trimester can be hit or miss, as moms are usually pretty tired, but most women are very aroused during the second trimester due to the increased blood flow in their body."

"Glad to hear." I smile, happy I don't have to become celibate for the next eight months.

"Do you have any questions, Tori?" her doctor asks.

"I don't think so. I've been reading up as much as possible these past few weeks, but I'll send a message in via the portal if I come up with one I can't find the answer to."

"Sounds good. I'll see you back in a month. Congratulations, again," Dr. Morgan says before she steps out of the room. Tori gets dressed, and we head down the hall to the ultrasound area. The technician is waiting for us outside her room, so we go right in.

"At eight weeks, we perform the ultrasound as a transvaginal one. I know you just had to get dressed in the exam room, but I need you to get undressed again, this time from the waist down, then have a seat on the table, and you can drape this over your lap. I'll step out and be right back," the tech tells her.

I sit next to the table and take her clothes as she undresses again. "I didn't realize I'd be getting two peep shows coming to the doctor's with you today," I tease her.

She just rolls her eyes at me and shakes her head, like she can't even deal with my smart-ass comments.

"All ready?" the tech asks as she cracks the door open.

"Yes," Tori tells her.

She steps back in and gets situated at the machine. She pulls out a long dildo-looking wand and covers it with gel. "I'm going to hand this to you and have you insert it inside your vagina. Once it's in, I'll grab the handle, and we can get some images of your baby. Sound good?"

"Yep," Tori tells her. I grimace at the size of the thing. It's good women have babies and not men, as I'd go running if someone wanted to shove that up me.

The large TV screen on the wall in front of us is filled with what looks like static TV. But apparently, it's Tori's insides.

"Right here is your uterus," the tech tells us. "And this, right here, is your baby. The flicker is his or her heartbeat," she says and hits a button, and the whooshing sound of a heartbeat fills the room. The sound brings tears to my eyes. I glance at Tori and see she's also crying. I grab her hand and bring it to my lips.

"We created that, babe," I say.

"I'm measuring you at eight weeks and one day," the tech says.

"Right on schedule," Tori comments.

"Good. I'll just snap a few pictures for you and print them out, and you'll be good to go," she tells us.

Tori gets cleaned up, and we head out, stopping at the checkout desk to pay her co-pay and make her next appointment.

This is really happening. We're having a baby. I slip my hand into hers, linking our fingers as we make our way out of the office.

CHAPTER 19
TORI

Seven months later

"Aiden!" I cry out. I'm in the bathtub, trying to relax. I've been having Braxton Hicks contractions for weeks now, but today they're almost unbearable.

"I'm here," he says, stepping into the bathroom.

"I don't think these are fake anymore," I tell him. "They hurt so bad," I cry.

"Do you want to head to the hospital?" he asks.

"I don't know what I want, other than this baby to be on the outside," I cry out as another contraction hits me. "Fuck, I think I need to push," I tell him as I look down and see the tub fill with a bloody liquid.

"Shit, I think you're about to have the baby," he says, going white as a ghost.

He leaves the bathroom, but returns a second later, this time with his cell.

"9-1-1, what's your emergency?"

"My fiancée is in labor. I think she's about to deliver our son," he tells the woman on the other end.

"Okay, Sir, let me get an ambulance on the way," she tells him. I cry out with another contraction and can't stop the urge to push.

"She's definitely in labor; I can see the top of his head," I hear him tell the lady.

"Okay, where is she at?"

"In the bath. She was soaking in there because it has helped in the last few weeks to calm her Braxton Hicks."

"It's a good place for her to be. Can you put me on speakerphone so you can assist her if the baby comes before the paramedics get there?"

"You're already on speaker," he tells her as he sets it down and hangs over the side of the tub. "You're doing so good, Tori," he tells me as I push again.

"His head is out," he tells her.

"Okay, can you see if the cord is around his neck at all?"

"I don't see it," he replies as he reaches down to feel.

"Good. Okay, gently pull him the next time she pushes, and he should fully come out. You can place him on her chest. If you have one of those nose bulb sucker devices, go grab it to help clear his nose and mouth once he's fully out," she instructs.

I push again, and he does just as he's told. He places our son on my chest, and tears of joy, exhaustion, and love fall from my eyes.

"He's here!" Aiden calls out.

"Congratulations," the operator tells us. "The ambulance should be pulling in now. Can you step away to let them in?" she asks him.

"Yeah," he says, and I can tell he doesn't want to leave us.

"We're good, Go let them in," I tell him.

"Paramedics are here," I tell the operator.

"Good. Congratulations. I'll just stay on the line so I can give them the official time of birth for the records, and then I'll let them take over," she tells me as our bathroom fills with two paramedics and three firemen.

I never thought I'd be okay with a room of four guys and one woman seeing me naked, but what other options do I have, seeing as I just freaking gave birth at home in the tub.

"Would you like to cut the cord," the female paramedic asks Aiden, and holds up a pair of funny-looking scissors.

"Yes," he tells her, and gets a little choked up as he does so.

They help me out of the tub and allow me to get dried off, then into some loose-fitting clothing before I sit on the stretcher so they can take us to the hospital to get checked out.

"You are welcome to ride with us or follow, so you have a car. Whatever you prefer," the paramedic tells Aiden as they settle the baby back in my arms.

"Call Ryker. I'm sure he'll come to pick you up," I tell him, not really wanting to be away from him during the ride.

"Can I bring our hospital bag in the ambulance?" he asks.

"As long as it can fit in your lap, sure," they tell him. He grabs the bag and our phones before heading to the ambulance.

"Can I have my phone?" I ask him when we're riding to the hospital. I snap a picture of our son on my chest. They wrapped him up in blankets and placed him back on my chest so he'd feel secure.

> Um, this happened just a few minutes ago in the tub. On the way to the hospital via ambulance now.

I shoot off the text with the picture to my best friend and parents, letting them know.

MOM

> Oh my goodness, he's so precious. But did you say AT HOME IN THE TUB?!

AVERY

> Oh my god! He's so cute. But what?!

I text my mom separately.

> Yes, in the tub. So far, the paramedics have said he's doing great. I'll update you once I've seen the doctor and we know if we'll be kept overnight at the hospital or discharged and sent back home. I'm not really sure how this works since he wasn't born in the hospital, but I assume we'll be admitted for the night.

I text Avery next.

> Thank you. It was a whirlwind; I'll fill you in later. Aiden will need a ride later, as he's in the ambulance with me; think Ryker can come get him once we know more?

> Absolutely. Just keep us updated. Congratulations. I love him already.

I give my phone back to Aiden, as we've pulled up to the hospital. They take me directly to labor and delivery rather than the emergency room.

Both of us are checked over and given a clean bill of health. Dr. Morgan comes in and helps with the delivery of my placenta, which hurt almost as badly as pushing out the baby.

"Good job playing doctor," she teases Aiden.

"It was scary, but Tori was the real rockstar," he tells her.

"Next time, when the contractions change, come in immediately."

"I was so tired of being told they were nothing, and I wasn't in labor," I tell her. We'd gone in three times in the last two weeks, thinking I was in labor, only to be sent home.

"The body is funny like that, but we now know you transition quickly. Many women will transition quicker and quicker with each delivery, so it's just something we should keep in mind for future pregnancies."

"How long will we stay in the hospital?" I ask.

"Even with a situation like yours, we like to observe

for a day, so at least tonight. If everything is going well with you and little man, you can go home tomorrow."

"Okay," I say, still shocked I delivered at home. "Are we allowed to have visitors?"

"Of course. They are welcome to come until eight," she says.

"I'll let everyone know they can come by," Aiden tells me once Dr. Morgan is gone.

"So, what are we naming this little man?" I finally ask Aiden once we've both had a chance to look at him and get a few uninterrupted minutes alone as a family of three.

"What are you thinking?" he asks as he looks longingly at our son.

"What do you think of Carter Aiden Fox?" I ask.

"I love it," he says, kissing me as tears fall down his face. "Happy birthday, Carter Aiden Fox. Daddy loves you, and I want to be the first person to tell you that you have the strongest mom. You're lucky to have her. I'm lucky to have her," he says to our son.

"I love you," I tell him when he looks back to me. "Thank you for knocking me up, even when I wasn't expecting it."

"Anytime, babe, anytime." He laughs and kisses me again. "Just, next time, tell me a little sooner that you're in labor so we can let the doctor deliver the baby and not me from the side of the tub."

"We'll have one hell of a story to tell for the rest of his life."

"That we will," he agrees.

CHAPTER 20
AIDEN

Six months later

I HOLD MY SIX-MONTH-OLD SON IN MY ARMS AS WE WAIT for his mom to come down the aisle to us. He's a squirmy little thing, now that he's mastered crawling this past week. He's into everything and always wants to be on the go.

"Carter, Mommy is coming," I whisper into his ear, hoping he'll be still for a few minutes, until I can pass him off and marry the love of my life. "See, there she is with Grandpa." I point down the aisle to where Tori and her dad are walking toward us. She's gorgeous in her gown and will be even more gorgeous when I strip her out of it later tonight.

Carter reaches for Tori as soon as she stops just a foot away from us.

"Hey, baby," she says, taking him in her arms and kissing his chubby cheeks. "Go with Grandpa," she tells him as she passes him off to her dad.

"You are fucking beautiful," I whisper so only she can hear.

Tori blushes and shifts her eyes to the minister only a few feet away from us, worried he heard me. Ryker chuckles from behind me, so I guess I wasn't as quiet as I thought.

The minister finally gets the ceremony started. I slip her wedding band on her finger and have to slyly wipe a tear from my eye before it slips down my cheek.

"By the power vested in me, I now pronounce you, man and wife. You may kiss your bride," the minister says.

I cup her cheeks and bring my lips to hers. "You're stuck with me for a lifetime, now." She laughs against my lips, and I take the opportunity to slide my tongue along hers, taking this kiss from PG to R in seconds.

Ryker clears his throat behind me, and I take the hint. Save the rest for the bedroom. "Damn, I think I might have gotten pregnant from that kiss." Ryker chuckles.

"Damn straight," I turn and tell him before I lead my wife down the aisle and to the reception.

"ARE YOU READY TO GET OUT OF HERE?" I ASK TORI. I WAS ready to leave hours ago, but was told I couldn't skip my own wedding reception.

"I suppose." She smirks.

"Woman, don't tease me. I need to be inside you, ASAP," I whisper into her ear as I pull her into me. I make sure she can feel how hard my cock is as it presses against her abdomen.

"I'm all yours, forever," she says.

We say our goodbyes to everyone. It takes Tori a good ten minutes before she's ready to leave Carter for the night, mostly because this will be our first night away from him since he was born.

"He's in good hands," I remind her. "Your parents are more than capable of watching him for the night, and they're staying at our place, so they'll have every-thing they could possibly need for him."

"He's still my baby, and I'm allowed to miss him," she pouts from the passenger seat.

"Don't worry, babe, I'll keep you well occupied all night. You won't have a worry in your body." I smirk as I drive us across town to the hotel we booked for the night. We plan on taking a honeymoon once Carter is a little older and not still nursing.

"Are you trying to knock me up again, husband?" she asks, rolling the word husband out. I like the sound of her calling me that.

"Are you giving me the green light to do so?" I ask.

"Part of me says to just pop out all the kids we want, close in age, so we're over the sleepless night phase in a shorter amount of time, but the other part of me says to space them out so my body has some recovery time between them."

"I'm happy to just practice." I shoot her a wink. "Or we could not really try, but also not prevent, and see what happens."

"We could do that. I haven't even gotten my period

yet, since Carter was born, which is normal when breastfeeding. So it might take us awhile anyways, or at least until he's done."

"If you're giving me the green light to ditch the condoms, I'm all over it," I tell her.

"You can ditch the condoms," she confirms.

"Hell yes!" I cheer as we pull into the valet line at the hotel. I hand over the keys, and they give me the tag for tomorrow.

I clasp my hand with Tori's as we make our way into the hotel and up to our suite. They have left a bouquet of roses, a tray of chocolate-covered strawberries, and a bucket of champagne on ice on the desk, along with a card congratulating us on our marriage.

I pop the cork on the champagne, pouring two glasses before handing one to Tori.

"To my beautiful wife, may you always know how much I love and cherish you. You came into my life when I least expected to find you and gave me a hard time when I tried to woo you, but I wouldn't change it for the world. I love your determination, how you give your everything when it is important to you, and how you love with all your heart. I love you, Tori Fox. Thank you for giving me my son and making me the happiest man alive."

We clink glasses and down the champagne before I take my wife to bed for the first time.

READY FOR MORE SHOCKWAVES? TRISTAN - THE 'FOREVER' bachelor is up next! You can grab his HEA on your favorite retailer today!

DID YOU LOVE AIDEN AND TORI? A REVIEW ON YOUR preferred platform helps authors reach new readers! Please consider leaving one today.

COMING SOON

To find out what's next from Samantha, please visit her website at samanthalind.com

ALSO BY SAMANTHA LIND

Indianapolis Eagles Series

Just Say Yes ~ Scoring The Player

Playing For Keeps ~ Protecting Her Heart

Against The Boards ~ The First Intermission

The Hardest Shot ~ The Game Changer

Rookie Move ~ The Final Period

Box Set 1 {Books 1-3} ~ Box Set 2 {Books 4-6}

Box Set 3 {Books 7-10}

Indianapolis Lightning Series

The Perfect Pitch ~ The Curve Ball

The Screw Ball ~ The Change Up

Lyrics & Love Series

Marry Me ~ Drunk Girl

Rumor Going 'Round ~ Just A Kiss

Standalone Titles

Tempting Tessa

Then You Came Along

When I Found You

Cocky Doc

Sweet Valley, Tennessee

Nothing Bundt Love

Nothing Bundt Forever

San Francisco Shockwaves

Ryker ~ Aiden ~ Tristan

Damien ~ Blake

Austin Fusion

Zack

ACKNOWLEDGMENTS

I have so many people to thank that I sometimes don't know where to start. I'll start with my family. Thank you for putting up with me when I had to disappear for an entire weekend to finish this book. There were many moments when I didn't think I'd actually finish on time, but with persistence, I made it happen.

Renee - I seriously couldn't do this without you! It is crazy sometimes how alike we think!

Author friends ~ Thank you for sprinting with me! You kept me going many days and nights.

My readers! You are the real MVPs here! Thank you for reading my books and loving my characters just as much as I do.

xoxo,

Samantha

ABOUT THE AUTHOR

Samantha Lind is a *USA TODAY* Bestselling contemporary romance author. When she's not dreaming up new stories, she can often be found with her family, traveling, reading, watching her boys on the ice or watching her favorite professional team (Go Knights Go!).

Connect with Samantha in the following places:

www.samanthalind.com
samantha@samanthalind.com

Reader Group
Samantha Lind's Alpha Loving Ladies
Good Reads
https://goo.gl/t3R9Vm
Newsletter
https://bit.ly/FDSLNL

facebook.com/SamanthaLindAuthor
x.com/samanthalind1
instagram.com/samanthalindauthor
bookbub.com/authors/samantha-lind

www.ingramcontent.com/pod-product-compliance
Lightning Source LLC
Chambersburg PA
CBHW061809190726

48289CB00007B/2135